COVENTRY

COVENTRY

HELEN HUMPHREYS

HARPERCOLLINS PUBLISHERS LTD
A PHYLLIS BRUCE BOOK

HarperCollins Publishers Ltd
2 Bloor Street East, 20th Floor
Toronto, Ontario, Canada
M4W 1A8

www.harpercollins.ca

Library and Archives Canada Cataloguing in Publication

Humphreys, Helen, 1961–
Coventry : a novel / Helen Humphreys.

ISBN 978-0-00-200726-9

I. Title.

PS8565.U558C68 2008   C813'.54   C2008-901825-7

HC 9 8 7 6 5 4 3 2 1

Printed and bound in the United States

Text design by Sharon Kish

FOR MY PARENTS

Rather than words comes the thought of high windows:
The sun-comprehending glass,
And beyond it, the deep blue air, that shows
Nothing, and is nowhere, and is endless.

—PHILIP LARKIN

NOVEMBER 14, 1940

The swallow arcs and dives above the cathedral. Harriet Marsh watches it flicker through the darkness ahead of her as she walks along the cobblestones toward the church. The bird moves in the night air with all the swiftness of sudden feeling, and Harriet stops at the base of the ladder, tracking the flight of the lone swallow as it shivers up the length of the church spire.

It is only when she is climbing the ladder that she remembers it is the middle of November. Swallows typically leave Britain by the end of October. This bird has stayed behind too long, will surely perish in the coming cold. Harriet stops halfway up the long ladder, looks for the bird, as though to warn it. The swallow has already disappeared.

The church roof is a dark tarpaulin hung from faulty stars.

"Bomber's moon," calls the boy from the roof of the chancel. His is the roof next to Harriet's and she can see him strutting up and down upon it. The lead tiles are slick with frost and she is afraid he will slip and fall, but she can't call out to warn him because she isn't meant to be here. She is wearing Wendell's overalls and his tin helmet. When he bundled his fire-watcher's uniform into her arms, he said, *No one will know you're a woman.* He said, *It's only for one night.*

The moon is full and bright, and the ground below the cathedral is white with frost. Harriet has never seen anything so beautiful. The ground glitters like the sea and smells of earthy cold.

There are four fire-watchers on the cathedral, each on a separate roof of the building. They all wear overalls and a tin helmet. Each one has a bucket of water, a bucket of sand, and a stirrup pump with a thirty-foot hose for directing water into the flames. Harriet hopes she won't have to use her stirrup pump because Wendell warned her it was really a three-person job, and he only gave her the most cursory of descriptions as to how it worked.

The moon has lit the city, and even though people have cinched their blackout curtains tight against the night, Harriet can clearly see the outline of every house. The brilliance of the moon unnerves her.

In Coventry, and in all the other British towns and cities,

people wait anxiously for morning. Since the beginning of September the Germans have been engaged in a massive air offensive against England. There have been raids on London, Southampton, Bristol, Cardiff, Liverpool, and Manchester. There has even been talk of a full-scale invasion.

Between the middle of August and the end of October there have been seventeen air attacks on Coventry. The most serious damage from the bombing raids was the destruction of the Standard Motor Works, but Harriet remembers more clearly the Sunday night in August when the Rex Cinema was hit. She had plans to see the new picture playing there that night—*Gone with the Wind*. She was late leaving her flat, and by the time she reached the cinema it had been bombed.

A major industrial town full of motor works and armament factories, Coventry is a prime target, and everyone who lives here knows this. Some people are so nervous of an air attack that they have taken to driving out of the city in the evening and sleeping in their cars in the countryside. Almost every night the air-raid sirens sound and there are fire-watchers walking the roofs of the city. The fire-watchers are old men and young boys. Twice a week, Wendell Mumby, the elderly man who lives in the flat below Harriet's, climbs up a ladder to this roof on the cathedral and keeps watch. This is the first night he hasn't been able to come, and all because Harriet washed the front hall of their building and Wendell slid in the passage and twisted his knee. He was afraid he wouldn't be able to climb the ladder to the cathedral roof and begged Harriet to take his shift instead.

I'm here because I feel guilty, thinks Harriet, as she walks gingerly across the slippery roof. I could fall off and break my neck, I could get blown up, all because I wet-mopped the front hall too vigorously.

"Look!" cries the boy on the chancel roof, and Harriet stops watching her feet and looks out at the glowing horizon. She hears the drone of planes approaching.

"Fire!" yells the old man on the south chapel roof.

From the cathedral roof Harriet can clearly see the neighbouring spires of Christ Church and Holy Trinity Church. She can see the dark hunch of roofs and the rivering streets between them, but after that the buildings fall off into shadow. The fire appears as a small orange smudge in the distance. It seems so far away that Harriet feels more relief than worry at first, until she remembers that most of the large factories in Coventry are on the outskirts of the city, right where the fire begins to bloom across the horizon line.

For a few minutes the fire-watchers live up to their name—four dark figures stamped against a moonlit sky, standing sentinel on the roof of the cathedral while the edges of the city begin to curl up and burn.

SEPTEMBER 20, 1914

The restaurant is dark and noisy. Harriet pauses in the doorway, trying to get her bearings. The last of the daylight leaks past her, and the people seated in the darkened room look over to where she stands with the door still open behind her.

They are two different places, thinks Harriet, stepping into the building. Outside, under the windy sky. Inside, with the tables holding a wreckage of glasses, the tilt of flame in the grate. One place is solitary. One place is social. Harriet is not sure which world she prefers, but Owen has already spotted her and is waving her over to a table in the corner where he sits with his parents.

Harriet can tell, even before anyone speaks, that the evening isn't going well. Owen's father has his hat on his lap, fingers worrying the brim. Owen's mother stirs her tea in tighter and tighter circles.

"Harriet," says Owen, his voice overflowing with relief. He springs to his feet and pulls a chair out for his wife. "I thought you'd never get here." His fingers brush Harriet's shoulders as she sits down, and even in that small touch she can feel his desperation.

"Have you ordered?" she says brightly. "Has anyone looked at the specials?"

There's a board on the wall at the end of the room with the daily specials chalked onto it in thick white letters.

Harriet knows that Owen's parents don't approve of what their son has just done, or of his marrying so young, but it still seems rude that they are sullen and unhappy every time the four of them have a meal out together. It isn't fair. Harriet presses her leg against Owen's under the table, and he presses back.

"Well, I'm famished," she says. "I hope there's steak and kidney pudding tonight."

"Mummy," says Owen. "What will you have?"

"I haven't had much of an appetite lately," says Owen's mother. She clatters her teaspoon down on her saucer.

"Nothing?" says Owen. "I know you like the liver."

"And you also know that I can't eat when I'm upset. You know that very well."

"Emily," says Owen's father sternly, as though reprimanding a child.

There's a silence during which Harriet tells herself not to

blurt out something she'll regret later, but she is only partially successful.

"Owen is doing this for all of us," she says. "And I've never been more proud of anyone."

Owen's father looks over at Harriet, and then at his wife. "She's right," he says. "If I was young enough I'd be in uniform myself."

Harriet tries to carry Owen over the threshold. He had carried her across the night before and done a better job of it. For someone so thin, Owen Marsh is surprisingly heavy, and Harriet sways and stumbles as she struggles with her husband into the sitting room of their rented flat on Berkeley Road. Last night he had carried her slung in his arms like a sleeping child, but she can only manage to clasp him around the waist and shuffle him along, a few inches off the ground.

"You'll never make it to the bedroom," says Owen. They're both drunk. After Owen's parents had left the restaurant, Owen, in his new uniform, had been stood a pint by practically everyone in the room.

"Of course I will," says Harriet, but she promptly drops him by the fireplace and then falls on top of him.

It is Owen's last night at home. In the morning he is to be shipped out to Europe. He will travel by train and ship to France and receive basic training there, behind the lines, before being sent into battle. Britain has only been in the war for a month, and Harriet and Owen have only been married for two. It all seems very fast. But she believes him when he says it will all be over by Christmas, and she is proud of her husband's ardent patriotism.

"Did a spaniel buy me a drink?" asks Owen. "Tonight when we were out, was that a spaniel in the corner by the bar?"

"Dogs have no money," says Harriet. "And no pockets to keep their money in."

"He had a spaniel nose, all turned up at the end."

"The end?"

"What?"

Harriet and Owen start giggling, and then fall asleep on the floor of the sitting room, flopped over each other like puppies in a litter. They wake to the dark and start to make love where they lie, on the patch of carpet in front of the cold fireplace.

The wool of Owen's uniform is stiff and unyielding. The buckle on his belt requires two hands to undo.

"I hope I never have to get out of this in a hurry," he says.

Their bodies fit together perfectly. When they kiss, their chins notch exactly against one another. It seems miraculous to Harriet that she has been given this much happiness, and even more miraculous that she is learning to take it for granted.

Owen kicks away the last pieces of his uniform and

rolls on top of Harriet, squashing the breath out of her. Over his shoulder she can see the sky lightening in the window, changing the shape of the darkness every few moments. Now it looks like the mane of a lion. Now it looks like a sail.

Owen's skin is soft and he smells of cigarettes and stale beer. Harriet licks his shoulder and then bites it, making him flinch. He has made the mistake of pinning her before she has removed her panties, and he is exerting great effort to do this now but not getting much result.

"Help me out," he begs, leaning his forehead, exhausted, against Harriet's. "Your uniform is even harder to get out of than mine."

———

In the morning, Harriet makes tea while Owen shaves. She brings her cup of tea from the kitchen, stands in the doorway of the bathroom, watching him. He is a careful shaver, thorough. At eighteen he has only been shaving for a few years, and he still treats it as though it is a privilege. He dips the razor in the basin of hot water after every stroke. Every few strokes he pauses to regard himself in the mirror, turning to the right and then the left to make sure he hasn't missed a hair. He is beautiful, with his dark hair and blue eyes, and Harriet thinks that he is much more beautiful than she is, and this thought suddenly makes her afraid.

"Your tea's getting cold," she says.

"How do I look?" Owen turns toward her, holding the dripping razor. He hasn't finished dressing, wears the trousers of his uniform but is bare-chested, his skin flushed from the steam in the bathroom.

"Lovely. Like a rose."

Owen grins. "Flatterer. How much time do we have before my train?"

Harriet grins back. "Now it's your turn to carry me over the threshold."

————

They have decided to treat the morning like an ordinary morning, but they can't find their usual banter as they walk to the station. Owen's hand is clammy in Harriet's, and she keeps tripping on the pavement. Her head hurts from the drink last night and the brightness of this morning. She barely sees where they are going.

The station is noisy, lively with soldiers and their families. There's a small military band playing at one end of the platform, and the train is already in, hissing and shaking like a live thing. The soldiers on board are whooping from the open windows, raucous with nerves and emotion.

Harriet grips Owen's hand tightly in her own. She had thought there'd be more time than this in which to say goodbye.

There are flags hanging above the station platform, above the cluster of families, each family encircling a young man in uniform.

"I wish your parents had come," says Harriet.

"I don't."

"But it's wrong for them not to see you off."

"It isn't, if one of them doesn't want me to go. Besides, the war won't last long. Everyone knows that."

Owen suddenly glances around in alarm at all the people on the station platform. "Harriet," he whispers. "I've never even been to Europe."

Harriet looks down at the kit bag he carries in his hand. She had slipped a pair of her panties in this morning, while he was busy shaving—those panties he had struggled so hard to take off her last night. Despite her anxiety it makes Harriet smile to think of Owen finding them there when he is in France.

"Do you love me?" she asks, but the train whistle blows and Owen doesn't hear the question. Or maybe he does. He drops his bag and embraces Harriet so passionately that she can't ask him again. For a brief moment she holds on to him. His body feels so thin and fragile under the bulk of his uniform. Then he sprints down the platform, looking for an open carriage door. The train pulls out of the station with one long, last blast of the whistle.

Outside the station, Harriet realizes that she doesn't quite know how to get home. Coventry is Owen's city, not hers, and they have only been living here since they married in July. She hasn't been to the station before, has always relied on her husband to navigate for them. Now Harriet stands at the corner of Eaton and Park, not sure which way to turn. She's too shy to ask the people pushing past her, so she looks up, finds the spire of St. Michael's, and heads toward that. The spire is the tallest shape on the horizon, and if she walks to the church surely she will recognize a landmark in the central section to guide her home.

———

Maeve rubs the back of her neck and thinks that the closer one is to something, the less one really sees of it. She lays her pencil down. She's getting a crick in her neck from looking up at the medieval spire, and she has realized she's too close to it to draw it properly. But if she's entranced by something, Maeve wants to be right next to it. She doesn't want to back up and allow other objects to fill her vision.

What a tease perspective is. She should have stuck with one of the arched windows.

She crosses the cobbled street to get a better angle on the spire and, sure enough, a young woman soon blocks her view of it.

"Pardon me," says the woman. "I wonder if you can help me? I'm looking for Berkeley Road."

The woman is roughly the same age as Maeve. She has dark hair pinned up under a straw hat decorated with flowers, and she's wearing a pale yellow dress, silk stockings, and shiny black shoes. She looks dressed up for a wedding.

"Sorry," says Maeve. "I'm not from here. I'm a visitor, same as you." She has come to Coventry to stay with her old school friend Charlotte, only to find out too late that Charlotte has invited Maeve to act as a cover so that she can spend all her time with her suitor, a soldier named Frederick Pearce.

"But I'm not visiting," says the young woman. "I live here. We moved north a few months ago so my husband could go into business with his father. The bicycle business," she adds. "He signed up, and I was just at the station, seeing him off."

It is a lot of information to give to a stranger. The young woman seems close to tears.

"You must be worried," Maeve says. They are perhaps the same age, but the young woman seems childlike, vulnerable. "I think I can help you out. I'm sure I remember seeing your road on my way down here." Maeve has lost her feeling for the spire anyway. She can always start again. She snaps her sketchbook shut and tucks her pencil behind her ear.

Harriet smiles at the gesture. "You look like a carpenter." She likes the easy gestures of this woman, the way she wears her hair bobbed short.

"Well, good," says Maeve. "I like being mistaken for someone useful."

They start off down Broadgate. The street is busy with shoppers. Maeve has no idea where Berkeley Road is, but she always tries to act with more confidence when she feels uncertain. She has successfully manoeuvred through her life thus far by doing this, so she strides out, forcing Harriet to break into a trot to keep up.

They pass a row of Tudor shops, each one supporting a top storey of black timbers and white plaster. There is a line of people outside the butcher's, and several delivery carts pulled by horses moving slowly down the street.

"Oh, look at that," says Maeve as a motor bus clatters by. "A double-decker. I haven't been on one yet, have you?"

The motor bus has only this year been introduced onto the medieval streets of Coventry. It is such a recent addition to city life in Britain that it is still a shock to see one.

"Shall we?" says Harriet, and the two young women look at each other and grin, grab their skirts and break into a run, chasing the bus down Broadgate until it stops. They clamber on, laughing and digging into their purses for their fares. "Berkeley Road," says Harriet.

They sit up top, in the open, under the bright sky. The bus lurches into gear and they shriek with delight, clutch on to the seat-back in front of them.

It seems to Harriet as though they are flying through the streets of Coventry. She throws her head back and watches the clouds, the blue blur of the morning. She can still feel the press of Owen's body against hers, the taste of their last kiss. She doesn't even know the name of the woman sitting beside her, but it doesn't matter. Owen will be home by Christmas. She is young and in love. Harriet, reckless with feeling, whoops from the top of the bus, the way the soldiers had sung out as the train pulled away from the station. It feels, for this moment, that it is she who is leaving Coventry, not Owen.

Maeve can't believe how high up they are, level with the top storeys of the buildings lining the road. She can catch glimpses of the furniture in the rooms above the shops. In one room she sees a painting of a horse on the wall. In another room she watches a woman hurry across to the window to stare out at the bus clattering past. It is as though Maeve has become a giant in a children's story, thundering along the ground, as tall as the tallest tree.

———

Harriet and Maeve tumble off the bus, giddy from their adventure. Maeve leads them around a corner, down a street, around another corner.

"There," she says triumphantly, and sure enough, when Harriet looks up she sees the sign for Berkeley Road.

"Would you come and have a cup of tea with me?"

"I'd love to," says Maeve, "but I have to meet my friend Charlotte for my daily briefing."

"Your what?"

"It's a long story." Maeve looks at Harriet and realizes that she hasn't done anything for ages that was as much fun as the ride in the double-decker bus, that these days in Coventry have been lonely ones for her. "Oh, bugger Charlotte," she says. "She'll just have to wait."

It feels strange to Harriet to walk into the flat and know that Owen won't be there, that she can't expect him back at the end of the working day. Suddenly the rooms seem full of him, and she pauses uncertainly before entering the kitchen.

"Do you think the war really will be over by Christmas?" she says.

"Why not?" Maeve likes the simplicity of the flat. There's no clutter. The only photograph above the fireplace is a wedding picture. She follows the straight line of the mantel to the straight line of the window ledge to the straight line of the worktop. "No one wants a war."

Harriet fetches the tea things. When she goes to the cupboard to get the cups, she sees Owen's teacup from this morning still sitting on the worktop. Perhaps she shouldn't have supported his decision to join up? She could have stopped him from going. He would have listened to her if she'd told him not to enlist. But all the young men were enlisting.

Maeve comes into the kitchen. "Your hat," she says. She reaches up and straightens it, her hands resting for a moment on Harriet's shoulders.

The touch calms Harriet. She closes her eyes, opens them again. The feeling of uncertainty has passed. She removes her hat, puts the dirty teacup from this morning into the sink, and places clean cups, a teapot, and a few slices of cake on the tray.

They drink their tea by the front window, side by side on the settee, as if they were still riding up high on the bus.

"What were you doing when I interrupted you this morning?" asks Harriet.

"I was drawing."

"What?"

"St. Michael's spire."

"Will you show me?"

Maeve hesitates. She has never shown anyone her drawings. She's not sure that she wants to. It's her private world. And the work isn't finished.

"Please," says Harriet, and she seems so genuinely interested that Maeve reaches into her bag and brings out the little sketchbook.

"It's no good," she says as she opens the book. "The perspective is completely off."

Harriet looks at the detail on the church spire, detail she has never noticed herself. Each piece of stone has been drawn by Maeve as either shadow or light. Her talent fills Harriet with wonder and admiration. The church looks more alive in the drawing than in reality.

"It's beautiful," she says. "It's even more beautiful than the real church."

"I should be off," says Maeve, but she is flattered by Harriet's response. She tears the sketch from her book, passes it over to Harriet. "Keep it," she says. "I'd like you to have it."

Harriet holds the drawing in both hands, looks at it carefully. "Thank you," she says. "Will you come and see me again?"

"Yes."

"Tomorrow perhaps?"

"Or the day after. No later than that."

"You'll remember how to get here?"

"I got us here this time, didn't I?"

When Maeve reaches the road, she turns and waves. Harriet waves back from the upstairs front window. It is not until Maeve is at the corner of the street that she realizes they never exchanged names.

———————

Charlotte has already eaten her lunch by the time Maeve gets to the café on Broadgate.

"I waited," she states. "And then I didn't."

Maeve has always admired the cavalier attitude of Charlotte Benson, but today it merely seems selfish.

"I'm not hungry anyway," she says. "I had tea and cake with a friend."

"What friend?"

"A new friend."

Charlotte raises an eyebrow. "A new friend?" she says. "Obviously I haven't been spending enough time with you. Tomorrow we'll take a walk in the countryside. Freddie has a chap he wants you to meet. And this weekend there's a dance. We can all go together."

"But I'm to go home on Sunday," says Maeve.

"So?" Charlotte waves for the waiter with a white-gloved hand. "You did come to Coventry to see me, didn't you?"

"Yes."

"And so you shall see a great deal of me between now and Sunday."

Maeve watches Charlotte's hand turning in the air. She wishes she'd asked the young woman her name so she could send a letter tomorrow and explain why she wouldn't be able to see her. She is surprised at how much she regrets this, and thinks of the thrill of the double-decker bus ride, and the even greater thrill of showing the woman her drawing. Maeve had felt at such ease with the young woman on Berkeley Road. It seemed that they understood the world in the same way, and that they would be good friends if given the chance.

MARCH 5, 1919

Harriet lays out her clothes on the bed. She is not sure how cold it will be. She is not sure if she should bring both a winter coat and her heavy cardigan that buttons up to the neck.

The taxi has been called for the morning. There is nothing left to do but sleep and rise and make her way to the station. Harriet stands by the front window, looking down into the garden. The moon has turned the path into a small silver river, slipping through the gate. She follows it with her gaze and suddenly remembers the young woman she met on the morning Owen left for France. How the woman had stood by the gate and waved up to Harriet. How she had given her the sketch of the cathedral. How she had promised to come and see her the next day, and had then disappeared.

Harriet turns abruptly from the window. She doesn't want to think of that woman, not now. She's just one more person who hasn't kept her promise; just one more person who hasn't returned to Harriet.

———————

The bus judders over the uneven ground. Harriet is thrown about in her seat, has to hold on to the seat in front of her in order to keep her balance, to keep herself upright. It is raining. The water falls in veils over the streaked glass, obscuring the fields of mud, the burned, skeletal trees that they pass on their way into Ypres.

The bus is full, and mostly women—wives, mothers, sisters of the soldiers who fought in the trenches here at the start of the war. No one speaks. Even last night, in the guesthouse in Poperinghe where Harriet and some of the other women were staying, no one had much to say. Grief, unlike love, seems to be a solitary experience.

They pass the ruins of a spinning mill, then a wooded area where the tops of the trees are all blown off and what remains are charred and splintered stumps, bare of leaves or bark.

Harriet still has the telegram she received two months after Owen left for Europe. When she was handed it solemnly by the messenger, on a crisp November day, at the door of the flat on Berkeley Road, she knew that it said one of three things. Her husband was wounded, missing, or dead.

When she opened it, with shaking hands, right there on the front door stoop, it said two of three things. Private Owen Marsh was missing, believed killed. Such a simple statement, with just one word between *missing* and *killed* to offer her the smallest flicker of hope. *Missing* in a place called Ypres.

How Harriet clung to that small pause between what she wanted, and what was probably true. For those first months after she received the telegram, she believed that Owen would walk into the flat at any moment. When that didn't happen, she believed that he was probably wounded somewhere, perhaps badly, and that they hadn't been able to identify him yet. She had heard stories of soldiers lying in military hospitals, suffering from wounds that left them unconscious and unable to identify themselves.

She waited for word, but none came. She went to the local war office every day to make inquiries. Then Harriet prayed to a God she had never really believed in, night after night down on her knees on the bare bedroom floor, her head resting on her clasped hands, the words rasping in her throat.

But nothing brought him back to her, and at the end of the war, when the death tally was done, Owen Marsh was simply one of nearly eight thousand soldiers who had perished on October 30, 1914, during the first battle of Ypres, simply one of ninety thousand British soldiers with, as the military reports put it, *no known grave*. A generation of young men gone.

The bus lurches to a stop and the doors swing open. There's a hesitation before people move from their seats. The rain is still pelting down and it is very cold. No one is dressed adequately. There's a hesitation, and then an old woman stands up slowly and they all rise.

Harriet steps off the bus and hunches her shoulders against the rain. She has forgotten her umbrella. It feels petty to mind getting wet, but she does mind. She walks purposefully down the road and into the ruined city.

———————

The Belgian city on the border of France had once been prosperous and had boasted many fine houses, many grand buildings and churches. It had a magnificent cathedral. The Cloth Hall was an enormous market for the buying and selling of every kind of fabric—wool, lace, linen, cotton. It had been built around a rectangular courtyard, and it was so vast that on the ground floor alone there were forty-eight doors to the outside. The river once ran through the town and allowed the boats carrying merchandise to sail right up to the warehouses to unload.

Now the main street of the city is entirely flattened. There isn't a building in Ypres that hasn't been affected by the shelling, that isn't either missing, or wounded, or destroyed.

Only because Harriet has seen pictures of Cloth Hall does she recognize what's left of it. It has been shelled to almost nothing. Parts of two walls remain, ragged towers of brick. The once impressive bell tower is a crumbling wreck, and what once were the two interior floors are now a mound of rubble filling the cavity between the walls, rubble as high as a small hill.

The cathedral is an endless plain of broken stone and dust, with several small portions of wall jutting up from the debris like tombstones.

Harriet walks through the city streets. The rain plasters her hair to her scalp and starts to run down the back of her neck. The other people who have been on the bus are reading their guidebooks, for there is a sombre guidebook that has been published for the thousands of people who travel here to see the ruins.

Harriet pulls her coat tighter around her. The mud is making it hard to walk, and she has no clear idea of where to go. She had been anticipating this moment for so long, this moment when she would be able to go to the place where Owen had last been; but now that she is here, she doesn't know what to do.

The dead men are nowhere to be found, and so it seems that they are, in fact, everywhere. There is no guidebook for that.

No one knows that Harriet has made this journey. She is estranged from her own family and has been for years, and Owen's parents, despite making a strained effort to be polite to her when she was married to Owen, have retreated into their own grief. They would think it ghoulish that she had travelled here to find the ghost of her husband. They dislike a display of feeling, prefer emotion to be securely locked away, like the good bone china they keep in the mahogany bureau in the parlour.

Yesterday the bus tour travelled to nearby Hooge, a village that had been completely obliterated. All that was left was the wooden signpost with the word *Hooge*. There was a small British cemetery there, containing about two thousand graves, on the western ridge above the vanished town; no grass, no trees, just tight rows of simple wooden crosses planted in the dirt. The names of the dead soldiers and their rank were painted on the crosses in white.

How Harriet envied the women who knelt in prayer in that small cemetery, weeping at the graves of their husbands. How she envied their laying of flowers on the graves, the way they ran their hands over the contours of the crosses. One woman laid her forehead against the top of her husband's marker, the way Harriet remembers Owen laying his forehead against hers. Harriet had to turn away at that.

Now, she huddles in a corner where two ruined stone walls meet. "Owen," she says out loud, just to hear his name here. "Owen."

She is past tears. She is past believing in his safe return. She is past love. She says his name into the falling rain, rubs the back of her knuckles against the stones until they bleed, and then she feels stupid and stops.

They are to stay the night in Ypres, in one of the small hotels that have sprung up to support the tourists who pour into the city. This afternoon they are to visit some of the remaining trenches and the wooded area where the soldiers would wait to be reunited with their regiment if they had become separated from it.

Harriet could never have imagined this much destruction. It seems unreal. She thinks of all those days and nights when she foolishly believed that Owen was still alive. Being here now, she knows absolutely that he is dead.

He is everywhere. He is nowhere. The blood on her knuckles is the brightest thing in this landscape. His name tastes like smoke in her mouth.

———

Owen had time to write Harriet only one letter before he was *missing, believed killed.* Before that letter she had received a regulation postcard. The postcard had lines already written on it that the soldier was supposed to cross out if they didn't apply to him. The lines that Owen had crossed out sent a chill through Harriet when she received the card.

I have been admitted into hospital.
I am sick and am going on well.

I am wounded and hope to be discharged soon.
I have received no letter from you for a long time.

What he left as his message was the simple and entirely banal *I am quite well. Letter follows at first opportunity.*

The letter, when it came, a mere week before the telegram arrived, was surprisingly vivid. Harriet had never known Owen to be much of a talker, let alone much of a writer, and she felt both comforted and alarmed by his letter. She was grateful that he hadn't tried to spare her his experience by engaging in reminiscences of their life together, or inquiries into how she was getting on at home. He still wanted to offer himself to her, even if just with words—and for this she was glad. But the man who wrote this letter to her was also not a man she felt she knew, and it alarmed her to think how much there still was to learn about her husband.

Harriet has brought Owen's letter with her to Ypres. But she has read it so many times that, even standing in the mud-filled trench, she can bring it back word for word.

Dearest Harriet,

Well, I'm writing from the trenches within hearing distance of the Germans; they are in fact only 25 yards away. It is daylight and a beautiful day and I've just had a good sleep in a sort of covered hole. There is nothing but sandbags all around, and a crater nearby full of dead matter. Yes, the stink is awful and the Germans have a nasty habit of stirring the bowl and keeping it good and fresh. However, in spite of all this, I feel unaccountably happy.

The Germans tried to bomb us out last night, but of course failed. This is the second time in this trench that I have helped to repulse the raiding enemy.

I'm now writing under candlelight in a foul-smelling dug-out which is fairly safe from shellfire. It must be at least 11 p.m. and my turn for guard comes at 12, for we only sleep by day.

Whatever happens, you must not believe that the Germans are worse than us. The regiments who opposed us just recently in Ypres were as human as could be to our wounded, even more so than we were to them. One fellow, having been wounded in the head during the night fighting lost his way, and hardly having the strength to stand, made for the nearest trench, or what was left of it. Just before he was about to jump in, he saw Huns crouching beneath him, and believing himself undetected, was about to turn back, when one of the Germans, seeing his wound in the head, immediately spoke in English and comforted him. The wounded man, feeling so weak, accepted and allowed himself to be helped into the trench. Then the German undid his cup and gave him water, laid him down *and sacrificed his coat. Soon afterwards the Germans evacuated this section, and when this man came to, he saw British soldiers carrying him out on a stretcher. As soon as he could he told his benefactors the story and showed them the cup that the German had allowed him to keep. I saw this mug. Many of our wounded have been found covered with coats.*

On the other hand, it is a recognized fact by both sides that when charging, enemy wounded left in the rear are killed to prevent any chances of their sniping.

The morrow morning: I am writing in a ruined church, on an improvised table, and I am facing what was once a garden. The sun is shining, the sky is blue, and a cooling breeze is blowing into my face. What a difference, what a contrast to the stagnant fire-swept, shell-torn battlefield, where all a man can do is to hug the earth and rot in dirty holes, and to inhale the filthy thick air.

The letter ends there, in the middle of the page. Owen has hastily scrawled a line of *x*'s and *o*'s for hugs and kisses, signed *Love,* and then written his name. Because the letter was completed over the course of three days, Harriet knows it was a struggle to write.

Harriet had never known him to write so beautifully. Early on in their courtship he had written her a few letters, but they were all of the *I can't wait to see you* variety—short, impatient declarations. This letter, even though it had taken three days to write, felt as though Owen had spent time with the words, had been careful in a way Harriet had not expected of him.

Harriet thinks how that letter has both stopped her from hating the Germans and has given her a small taste of the man she was just beginning to know, how because there is no body to grieve, it is the last thing she will ever have of her husband—those words on that page.

———

Sanctuary Wood is a torn piece of earth with a few upright dead trees, standing like burned matchsticks in the dirt. It is impossible to imagine that it was once a wood filled with flowers and birds and that particular kind of light that sifts down through the leaves overhead. In the early days of the war, it had offered a brief respite from the fighting to the men who had become lost in the maze of muddy trenches and had climbed out, retreated back to the wood, and waited there to reunite with their regiments.

"It wouldn't have been a wood for very long," says the woman beside Harriet as they walk between the blackened trees. "For most of the war, it would have looked like this."

Harriet wonders if Owen was ever in the wood. She had thought, on the journey across the Channel, on the journey into Ypres, that she should try to find the church where he had penned the last fragment of his letter. She hadn't anticipated the utter devastation of the city.

"Do you know where your husband died?" she asks the woman.

"Brother," says the woman. "My younger brother, Robert. And no, I don't know where he died. He is missing."

Believed killed, thinks Harriet. They move out of the trees, look across to the rest of the group gathered near the trenches. The rain is still falling. Harriet can feel it creeping over her skin under her clothes. "What was he like?" she asks. "Your brother."

The woman turns and looks at Harriet. She's wearing a mackintosh pulled up almost to her ears. Her hair is limp and stuck to her skull. Harriet can see the muddy hem of her black dress at the bottom edge of the mackintosh. It looks like the same black dress she herself is wearing.

"He was a lot of fun," the woman says. "Always up for a lark. He made me laugh. And your . . . ?"

"Husband," says Harriet.

What can she say about Owen now? It feels to Harriet as though she never knew him, he has slipped so far out of reach despite all her efforts to hang on to him. Even though she keeps a photograph of their wedding day beside her bed, she can't remember his smile, or the look in his eyes when he laughed, or the sound of his voice. She knows he liked

36

bicycles, but that seems a ridiculous thing to say. He's been missing for so long now that all she can really be sure of is what he meant to her.

For all her efforts Harriet can't really remember Owen very well. His memory has been worn thin from use, like a patch of cloth rubbed too vigorously and too often. She has her ideas of him and of their happiness, but at this point the reality of him has been subsumed into her own need to remember him in a certain way. In real life he would never have bent to her will, but now that he's dead she can do whatever she chooses with him. This knowledge sickens her, but she is also powerless against it.

She turns away from the woman without answering her question and moves out of Sanctuary Wood to rejoin the rest of the tour group.

———————

That night in the hotel, Harriet can't sleep. She lies fully clothed on the narrow guest-house bed, listening to the women crying through the thin walls that separate the various rooms. The high-pitched murmuring sounds like birds in the trees.

She is thinking of the mud dragging her feet to ground, of the black trees, sharp as spears, standing upright in the small patch of earth that had once been a wood.

She gets up, lights a candle, and carries it over to the

chair by the fireplace. There are a few books on the mantel. She trails a finger over their spines.

She puts the candle holder on the floor, gets down on her hands and knees in front of the fireplace. She tries to pray, but the words have left her. The fire has only recently gone out. She puts her hand into the grate and pulls out a warm half-burned lump of coal. She makes a mark with it on her arm, then another on the tiles around the fireplace.

Harriet gets up and goes into the hallway. People have put pieces of cardboard by the doors to their rooms for the muddy boots. She carefully lifts her boots off the cardboard, and carries it back into the room. She gets down, once again, on the floor by the hearth and turns over the cardboard. She picks up the piece of coal and begins to draw.

Later, much later, when she is back home in England, she will write what will become the first of what she comes to call her *descriptions*.

For hours, for no reason that I could imagine, I drew black swans. Hunched over a piece of cardboard on the floor of the hotel room, the coal softening to dust on this surface beneath me.

What I wanted was the simple pleasure of seeing you again. But you didn't come, couldn't come. I don't know how to make you return to me.

But I did come to know the black swan. I knew the long snake flex of its neck, knew that the shape of the body was a leaf, a wing, an open hand, the human heart. I fastened these images to paper, called them swan. And then I rose, black dust dripping from my hands, my arms spread empty to the empty sky, as I walked out through broken streets feathered with shadow—darkness lifting me home.

NOVEMBER 14, 1940

Harriet Marsh is certain of very few things. As she washes the front hall of her building, she takes an inventory. She used to believe in love, but she has worn that down to nothing. Every time she visits the memory of Owen it is foggier, farther away. She used to believe her writing was a way to stay connected to her dead husband, but years of typing up her descriptions after work in the cold offices of Bartlett's Coal Merchants have left her emptied out of feeling. She is tired of trying to hammer a moment shut with words. All she has left is the outdoors, and most days this is a noon-hour head-down tromp through the muddy farmers' fields that surround Coventry, where she tries desperately to be moved by a single dog rose or the flower of the black-thorn hedge.

Nothing holds its truth for long enough. Home leaves us, not the other way around, she thinks. And what are we meant to do when we come to know that?

———————

Harriet is disappointed by the new war but not devastated by it. She won't suffer as she suffered in the first war. This war does not have the power to do that to her. She sullenly capitulates to the rationing, doesn't mind eating the horse meat—although the yellow fat that rivers through it is disgusting. She has even eaten the new meat product called snook, which is a rather horrifying cross between Spam, corned beef, and rubber. It has a grey appearance and smells like fish gone off.

Harriet endures the talk of raids and bombardments, listens to Wendell Mumby's endless fantasies of saving the entire nation single-handedly from enemy capture. She has sewn blackout curtains for the flats in her building, painted her bicycle black, helped her neighbours dig a three-foot pit in their back garden for an Anderson bomb shelter. As if that would save them.

But this war, although not equipped to cause emotional pain to Harriet, is more dangerous to her physical well-being. The Germans are intent on flattening London and other major British cities. Having recently conquered Holland, they can use airbases there and in France to fly back and forth across the Channel, carrying their deadly cargo of bombs. Since September 7, there have been bombing raids against London for fifty-seven consecutive nights. Churchill, instead of being persuaded by these attacks to negotiate peace, has appealed to the British public to stand firm against the onslaught. Everyone is trying to be courageous. The most common thing Harriet sees in the boarded-up shop windows is the hastily scrawled sign *Business as usual.*

The RAF is countering with raids against Berlin and other German cities, but it is no match yet for the steady wave of German bombers. The RAF targets are too far inland. The most it can hope for, at this point, is to engage with the enemy planes over the Channel, when the Luftwaffe is on its way to bomb England.

Harriet admires Churchill's stubborn refusal to admit defeat, but she also fears privately that the Germans are winning the war, and that it won't be long until London is completely destroyed, although she dares not say this to anyone. And, if London is destroyed, England will fall.

———

"Bomb!" yells the boy on the chancel roof.

Harriet hears the drop and sizzle, can see that the object that has fallen from the sky to the roof is too small to be a bomb. It looks no bigger than a rubber ball. She can smell the singe of it from her roof.

"It's not a bomb," she says, and the boy turns back toward her voice from where he had skittered off in the direction of the ladder.

"You're a woman," he says.

Harriet Marsh coughs and lowers her voice. "No, I'm not," she says hopelessly. "I'm Wendell Mumby."

The boy laughs, then he crouches on the chancel roof.

"What is it?" says Harriet.

"It's a bird, Wendy," he says. "It's a bird, and it's fully cooked. It must have flown through the fire." He nudges the charred body of the swallow with his foot until it rolls off the edge of the roof.

Perhaps the fire on the horizon is so great that the flames reach right up into the sky, as high as the flight of a bird. This is what Harriet thinks but does not say. She also thinks the glow of the fire is brighter, closer than it was mere minutes ago. All these autumn nights Wendell Mumby has fire-watched on the roof of this cathedral and never had to deal with a fire. He assured Harriet she would have the same experience. She feels angry at Wendell for misleading her; and then she realizes she is feeling angry so she won't have to feel afraid. But it's no use. She feels afraid anyway.

As if to give voice to her fear, the air-raid sirens start to wail. The thunder of the German bombers rolls across the sky.

The first incendiary bomb falls on the chancel roof. It

is long and cylindrical, like a firecracker, and the moment it makes contact with the roof it blossoms into flame.

"Sand. Use the sand," yells the fire-watcher on the south chapel roof.

The boy douses the fire with his bucket and kicks the extinguished flare off the roof.

An incendiary drops on the roof of the south aisle, above where the massive pipe organ sits. A firebomb hits the roof above the nave. This one burns through the lead tiles. Men are climbing from the ground, up the ladders, and onto the roof of the cathedral with extra buckets of sand and water. Someone splits the roof with an axe and someone else pours sand onto the burning wooden rafters below. The stirrup pumps are married to the buckets of water. The water falls in veils above the flames.

The fire-watchers know that the cathedral roof is really two roofs. There is an inner ceiling of panelled oak and an outer wooden roof covered in lead tiles. There is a space of eighteen inches between the two roofs, and if a fire catches and burns in this space, there will be no way to extinguish it.

Harriet helps haul the buckets of sand and water up onto her roof. Her tin helmet knocks against her forehead and tips down over her eyes. She pulls it off and lays it on the roof by her feet. A shower of incendiaries falls on the cathedral and Harriet can see smoke pouring from the holes where the axe has split through the tiles.

There are more men on the roof. There is a rush of buckets, a spray of sand. The smoke seems to be diminishing and Harriet thinks that perhaps the fire is under control.

And then another cascade of incendiaries hits the roof.

"Get off. Get down," the men are yelling to one another.

"Call the police. Call the fire brigade," they shout to the waiting crowd at the base of the church. "The cathedral's on fire."

There is no sound of approaching fire trucks, only the yelling of the fire-watchers and the crackle of the fire on the church roof. And above that, the surge of bomber engines as the planes continue coming.

Harriet has lost sight of the boy from the chancel roof during the fire-fighting, but she finds him on the ground when she scrambles down the ladder. He's by himself, a little way away from the building, watching the fringe of flame feather along the roofline. He seems frozen, but his hands are trembling.

"What can we do?" he asks. "How can we stop it, Wendy?" He rubs his head nervously.

The job of a fire-watcher is to alert the rescue services to fires and to extinguish any fires in their area. There is no procedure for what happens after the fire is raging out of control.

All around them Coventry is slowly catching fire. The incendiary bombs are falling not just on the cathedral but on

48

all the buildings around the cathedral, all the buildings in the old section of town.

Harriet's flat is away from the centre of Coventry and she is wondering how she will get back there. She is afraid for Wendell and for her cat, Abigail, whom she left curled up contentedly in the armchair by the airing cupboard. But as to her own safety, she is surprised at how little she cares.

"I'm Harriet," she says. "Not Wendy."

"James," says the boy. "James Fisher. But everyone calls me Jeremy."

"Jeremy Fisher, like the frog?"

"My mother used to read me that story," says the boy. "When I was young."

He still seems like a boy, has the quick, skittish movements of a child, but his voice is the voice of a man, and when Harriet looks at him she sees that he is as tall and broad as any man.

Perhaps if she talks to him he will stop trembling. "I always thought the Jeremy Fisher story was a little sad," says Harriet. She likes the Beatrix Potter stories herself and is too ashamed to admit that she dips into them regularly. She finds the escapades of the small animals comforting. Jeremy Fisher goes fishing for minnows and then is almost eaten by a trout. But the trout spits him out. He doesn't like the taste of the frog's mackintosh.

"There's that drawing of Jeremy Fisher crawling up the riverbank, his mackintosh in tatters," says Harriet. "This is the awful moment when he realizes his life is not what he thought. He has been operating in the world as a predator and now he understands that he is really prey." What a strange conversation to be having, but he seems to be calmer now.

The boy is quiet for a moment. "I hope my home hasn't been hit," he says.

"I'm sure it hasn't." Harriet is astonished to find that she wants to protect him, this young man with the name of a frog in a children's story. She thinks again of Wendell Mumby, home in front of the fire with his leg elevated. He has been waiting all autumn for some action and now he will miss everything.

But the factories of Coventry are right beside the housing districts. The bombs falling on Triumph Engineering, Daimler, Rover, and Singer Motors are also falling on the streets next to them—streets full of houses, and the houses full of people at this time of night, unless they have managed to reach the shelters. It is only a matter of time, thinks Harriet, before the centre of the city is on fire. The ground that she and Jeremy stand on, here at the base of the burning cathedral, is no safer than the factories on the edge of the city.

———

Maeve tries not to drink her pint too quickly. She hasn't eaten anything this evening and she doesn't want the beer to go to her head.

It's dark in The Coachman, the blackout curtains stretched tight across the front window. Even during the day, with the curtains open, the window glass is taped so it won't blow out in a blast. There is so much tape across the window that it might as well be a curtain, so little light gets through. But the regulars are there, as usual, at the same tables. There's the familiar shuffle of chairs and voices.

Maeve is sitting at a small table in a nook by the fireplace. The only real light to see by is the firelight, and it is unreliable. She looks down at her sketchbook, at the drawing she has started and stopped half a dozen times now. It would have been wiser to stay home this evening. She would have had a better chance of getting this done.

All around Maeve are bubbles of conversation, the slap of glasses against the wooden tables, the loud voice of the publican as he shouts down the length of the bar to alert a patron to the pint he has just poured. If Maeve had stayed home, she may have been able to execute her sketch, but she would have been alone. On the nights when her son is on duty, Maeve likes to come to the pub. It feels better to be around other people in case the air-raid sirens go off, even if she never feels like talking to anyone while she's there.

Maeve just likes to sit quietly and listen to the laughter and chatter around her. It makes her feel less isolated.

Maeve has not lived long in Coventry. She came north because there were jobs on offer, and because it had seemed unlikely, at the beginning of the war, that there would be any threat to the northern cities. Now, after endless raids, it is clear that Coventry is a prime target for the Germans. The motor and armament factories that lured Maeve and her son north have lured the enemy across the Channel as well. Still, they are relatively settled here, and travel is increasingly difficult in wartime, so Maeve is prepared to wait out the war in this town that she has visited before but where she never meant to live.

Maeve doesn't remember her childhood in the south of England very well. Her early life seems broken into vivid tableaux, each one seemingly unconnected to any of the others. She has trouble thinking chronologically anyway, never thinks, *When I was seven* but rather *That colour blue is the same colour blue as the sky out my nursery window that morning I woke up to the dogs barking.* She is caught on these small hooks of the past all the time, has difficulty untangling herself from them.

The soft green of the grass in her front garden this evening, shining in the moonlight, is the same green as the leaves Maeve used to post through her grandmother's letterbox at the country house. She picked them from a plant in the front garden, after she'd been turned out of the house to play, following tea. The leaves were as soft as bunny ears. Maeve rubbed them against her face before shoving them through the heavy steel flap of the letterbox. The elderly golden retriever that she'd been sent out to play with watched her disapprovingly from the open garage door. After a while Maeve was discovered and got into lots of trouble for decimating the front garden, but in the moments before that, when she was reaching up on her tiptoes to push the leaves through the metal slot, there was an immense feeling of satisfaction as she completed the task. Maeve can still recall that feeling.

"What are you drawing?" asks the old man at the table opposite. He has been watching Maeve since she first sat down, and she has been careful to avoid eye contact with him so she won't have to make idle chit-chat.

"Nothing," she says, which is a stupid answer, so she says, "Nothing much."

"What then?"

"A bird." Maeve looks down at the wings, the small smooth head, the scissored tail. "A swallow. There was one flying about in my street today."

"Impossible," says the man. "Swallows are long gone by now."

"It was a swallow," says Maeve. She is distracted by this man, whom she never wanted to talk to. She is tired of

England's population being made up now almost entirely of women, children, and the elderly. Old men in particular are too convinced of themselves, she thinks.

The swallow had sliced through the air outside her kitchen window, and she had followed it outside, watching the bird's sweet slide over her garden's stone wall. She had always liked the flight of the swallow. It was such a graceful bird. It made so many interesting shapes in the air.

"It was most likely a sparrow," says the man opposite, and before Maeve can respond with indignation, the air-raid sirens begin to wail. This is the eighteenth raid on Coventry since the middle of August and there is a weariness in the patrons as they rise from their tables and follow the publican down the cellar stairs.

———————

When Maeve was young, she'd had a book with a painting of Lady Godiva on a white horse, her hair carefully arranged to cover her naked body. The hair was so unnaturally long it suggested another creature. The woman, the horse, and the hair, all of these fascinated a young Maeve Fisher. This was her entire knowledge of Coventry.

But it was the visit in 1914 that had stayed with her, and she had been happy to move here this year, when there seemed to be no jobs anywhere else in the country. The time with the irritating Charlotte had seeded in her an appetite for independence. It took four more years to root, but she had been preparing herself the entire time for that glorious day when she would be free from expectation, from duty, from her parents' plans for her. It didn't quite happen the way Maeve had imagined it, but it happened all the same.

After her parents found out she was pregnant and she refused to divulge the name of the father so he could do the decent thing and marry her, Maeve's father told her to leave the family home. For years, her parents disowned her, and it is only recently that her father has decided he wants to see her again, and only because he is getting on in years and is worried about his place in the afterlife if he hasn't satisfactorily tidied up all his business here on earth before he dies. But Maeve isn't sure she wants to co-operate.

Those first months, the months after Maeve had left home but before Jeremy was born, were the worst of her life. Her friends, most of whom still lived with their parents, were unable to take her in. She had little money and no employment. She was too proud to beg for charity. Eventually, out of desperation she took a gamekeeper as a lover so she could stay with him in his cottage on an estate.

The gamekeeper's cottage was shrouded in ivy. Some of the windows were completely covered over and the inside of the cottage glowed green when the sun was shining. It was like being underwater. Maeve moved through the space that way, drifting from pool to pool, being borne along by a current of need or mood, whatever was strongest at a particular moment.

Her baby slept in a dresser drawer on the floor by the bed, and sometimes, when Maeve woke to the green light at the window, her son's cries sounded like the birds outside. The gamekeeper complained about the noise the baby made and the attention he demanded from Maeve.

She was always disoriented in that cottage. The inside was outside, and the outside was inside. The gamekeeper would leave dead rabbits flung down on the kitchen table for Maeve to prepare. Their legs would be tied together, but otherwise they still looked alive, lying there in the morning when she came down, their eyes open and watching her as she came into the kitchen. Even the dead rabbits were judging her and finding her wanting.

———————

Maeve is crouched in the cellar of The Coachman. It is damp and smells of old wood. She is sitting on a pile of burlap sacks with a cask on one side of her and the annoying sparrow man on the other side. Everyone is much more crowded here than they were upstairs. The publican and his wife have lit candles and placed them on top of the beer barrels. They illuminate the faces of the patrons in ghostly shadow. Maeve hugs her knees to her chest and huddles closer to the cask. The wood is rough against her cheek. She can still hear the wail of the air-raid sirens, but there is no reverberating echo to indicate that bombs are falling on the world above them.

"False alarm," says the sparrow man.

"No," says an old man across the room. "Jerry will be after the motor works."

"A quick and dirty raid," says the publican.

"Could last all night," says his wife.

"Bound to be a false alarm," says the sparrow man.

Maeve thinks longingly of her half-full pint and wishes she'd had the presence of mind to bring the beer down into the cellar with her.

She thinks of Jeremy, how she watched him walk up the road in his fire-watcher's uniform. How proud he seemed to be, doing his bit for the war effort. She worries constantly about him, her only son. But he will be safe tonight, she thinks. The cathedral is massive. There will be a shelter in the crypt, and he will be safe there. He is clever and resource-ful. He won't take chances.

She suddenly has an image of him not as the young man he is now but as the infant he used to be, squalling in her arms as she rocked him in the gamekeeper's cottage at night, trying to keep him quiet.

When we are safe, Maeve thinks, then Jeremy is a man. But when there is danger, he is my child again.

———————

Coventry Cathedral is the largest parish church in England—evidence of the wealth the city had once possessed. It is the literal heart of the city, known to everyone who lives there, the spire visible from every street. Even though she is not herself a believer in God, Harriet is always comforted by the magnificence of the cathedral, such an impressive monument to faith.

Now Harriet stands in front of the cathedral, helplessly watching it burn. There is a small crowd of people around her. She recognizes the provost, an important dignitary in the city. He is rushing about, ushering the last of the men down the ladders from the roof. The man standing on Harriet's left is crying. Someone else is cursing the *bloody Jerries*.

"There's the fire brigade," yells Jeremy, and Harriet turns to see a single fire truck lurch to a stop in front of the cathedral as the men unravel the hose and begin to wind it around the building. Length after length of hose is fitted together until, finally, a spray of water falls over the chancel roof.

There is a cheer at the sight of the water and then, just as it started, the water stops.

"We're doomed," says the man beside Harriet. "This is the end of Coventry."

"No," says Jeremy. "They're running lengths to the hydrant on Priory Street. The water will come back on."

But the water doesn't come back on.

"The mains must have been hit," says Harriet. It takes her a moment to realize the seriousness of this. With no water there will be nothing to stop the fires spreading throughout the city. The whole of Coventry will burn.

There is not much that can be salvaged from the cathedral—the altar cross and candlesticks, a silver chalice, a silver wafer box. From the high altar in the sanctuary—its cross and candlesticks, a wooden crucifix, the altar service books, the book of gospels. Everything has to be taken quickly from the smoke-filled rooms. Everything must be small enough to carry.

On the walls of the sanctuary are the colours of the 7th Battalion, Royal Warwickshire Regiment. They had been left in the cathedral at the beginning of the war, for safety's sake, and now they are torn from the walls and carried out of the burning church.

It is a small and sombre procession that hurries, under the colours of the Warwickshire Regiment, from the cathedral to the police station to deposit the valuables in the basement of the station. No one can think of a safer place, and yet all around the police station fires are burning and Harriet realizes that there really are no safe places in the city tonight.

She carries a pair of heavy silver candlesticks, one in each hand. They are warm against her skin from the waves of heat billowing through the streets.

Inside the police station men are rushing about, shouting at one another. Phones are ringing. A man sits at a desk repeatedly dialling his phone, until another policeman shouts to him that the lines out aren't working, only incoming calls are getting through.

"If the phones don't work, how will the rescue services know where the fires are?" says Harriet to the man in front of her on the staircase as they ascend, out of the basement.

"It's not the fires we have to worry about," he says. "It's the bombs. They light the fires so they can see where to bomb."

Harriet waits for Jeremy at the top of the stairs. He had carried the silver wafer box into the basement with both hands, holding it away from his body.

"It was burning me up," he says when he emerges from the cellar. "Just as if it had come from the oven."

He stands close to Harriet, looking around at the activity inside the police station. "I need to find my mother," he says.

"Where do you live?" asks Harriet. She feels oddly calm.

"Mayfield Road."

"That's near me," says Harriet. "I'm on Berkeley. We could go together." It would be quicker without the boy, but Harriet likes the way he has tucked himself against her, as though he somehow belongs to her. No one has ever sought her out for protection before. It makes her feel she is a better person than she knows herself to be.

"Yes," says Jeremy. "I'd like that. We only moved here this summer. I hardly know the city at all, and I certainly won't recognize it when it's burning." He still wears his tin helmet. There's a smudge of black across his cheek. He looks impossibly young, and Harriet realizes with a shock that he is probably the age she and Owen were when they married.

"Let's go then," says Harriet, and they weave their way through the frantic policemen and step outside into the chaos.

It is about a mile to Berkeley Road. The fires have made the streets as bright as day. Harriet moves tentatively down the front stairs of the police station. She can see great clouds of smoke swirling up the street, people flitting through the flames like moths. There's the shudder of buildings falling, and an overwhelming smell of cigars. How strange, Harriet thinks. It takes her a moment to realize that the tobacconist on the corner is burning.

"Let's stay to the centre of the road," she shouts. "It will be safer there. We won't be hit by falling debris." She can see the charred ribs of the timbers sticking out from the smouldering heap of rubble.

"Wear my hat," says Jeremy. He takes his tin helmet from his head and places it gently on Harriet's. He then offers his arm, and Harriet takes it, and they step carefully down the centre of Broadgate, as though they are a couple strolling out after dinner to gaze at the stars.

They make it to the end of the block before Jeremy stops. "Look up," he says.

Harriet looks up and sees four land mines drifting down under parachutes. They are lit from beneath by the fires, the soft, filmy hoods of light making the bombs seem like a school of jellyfish, not descending, but swimming up out of the darkness.

———

Just as the man at the police station predicted, the incendiaries are followed by bombs. The bombs in turn create fireballs. It is impossible to escape down Broadgate.

Harriet and Jeremy crouch in an alley between two buildings. They ran as fast and as far as they could before the land mines finished their dreamy drift down, but there was no time to get to a more secure place before one of them exploded. The noise is deafening and they can feel the rush of heat and air as it blasts through the street. The buildings on either side of them sway and tremble but do not buckle and fall.

Harriet feels detached, but when she adjusts Jeremy's helmet on her head she notices her hand is shaking. Jeremy seems frozen.

"We need to get to a proper shelter," she yells. A direct hit and the buildings they are crouched beside will collapse on top of them. "We're not far from Owen Owen. There's a concrete shelter in the basement there."

Owen Owen is the new pride of Coventry, a massive department store in the centre of the city, right on Broadgate. It has one of the largest public bomb shelters in its basement.

The brick wall of the building Harriet is leaning against is warm against her back. The wood inside is starting to groan and creak.

"I think this shop's on fire," she shouts. "We need to get out of here. Keep your head down." She grabs Jeremy's hand and pulls him along the alley toward the street.

———————

Owen Owen is burning. The acrid smoke rolling from the building makes it difficult to breathe. Harriet's lungs burn with the effort. A small crowd stands helplessly on the road outside the department store, watching the flames dance around the oven that the brick shell of the building has become.

"What about the people in the shelter?" asks Harriet. The man beside her shrugs his shoulders.

The Anderson shelter at the bottom of her neighbour's garden on Berkeley Road is too far. They need a place now.

"Where are the other shelters?" she asks the man. Jeremy has moved closer to the building to get a good look at the fire. Harriet can see his long, thin back up ahead of her. She is determined not to lose him.

"Where are they?" she demands.

"No need to snap at me," says the man. "Try the churches."

Harriet just wants to be off Broadgate now. The main street in the city is so obviously under attack as well. She pushes through the knot of people in front of her and grabs Jeremy by the collar.

"We're off," she says. "We're going to try the church around the corner."

Another bomb explodes. The ground rocks slightly beneath Harriet's feet and she has to scream to make her words heard above the blast. "We have to get out of here." She hauls Jeremy backwards, away from the burning shell of the building.

―――――――――

The sparrow man has started singing "Rule Britannia." He has a thin, reedy voice that spirals through Maeve Fisher. All around her, people stumble into song. The candles stutter with the sudden bursts of breath.

The air-raid sirens have stopped. The bombing has stopped. There is no sound from above. Surely it would be safe to go up now, even if the all-clear hasn't sounded? What about Jeremy? What if he has tried to come home rather than sheltering at the cathedral?

Maeve shifts on her pile of burlap. She feels damp from sitting on the floor. Just then there is an enormous thunder-clap and the building sways and settles, sways and settles.

Dust trickles down from the cellar rafters onto Maeve's face. The first explosion is followed by a second. Maeve can hear something tearing and splintering above her head.

"Looks like we'll be here a while," says the publican, and the whole room belts out the chorus of "Rule Britannia" all over again. This time, Maeve sings along.

———————

After Maeve left the gamekeeper, she was hired as a domestic in a big country house. The lady of the house took pity on Maeve's situation, and although Maeve didn't want pity, it served her well enough to be on the receiving end of it.

Maeve was well liked in the country house. Her cheerfulness made her popular with both the servants and the family. Consequently, Jeremy was looked after by everyone, shuttled around the estate like a parcel, and though at first Maeve worried when she didn't know where he was or whom he was with, she learned to trust that he was being properly looked after.

One summer a painter came to visit the estate and Maeve was asked to act as her personal assistant. The artist liked to paint from nature, but needed such a large amount of equipment to do this that Maeve ended up wheeling the easels, boxes, and brushes through the bumpy fields in the gardener's wheelbarrow. The painter's name was Marguerite, although later, after she'd left the estate, Maeve found out that her name was really just plain Margaret. She had long red hair that she kept tied up with coloured scarves. She smoked French cigarettes and swore as fitfully as the game-keeper when things weren't going well with her painting.

The summer as her assistant was the best summer Maeve ever spent. At first she read a book or picked wildflowers. But she soon tired of this and began to watch Marguerite. Then she began to ask questions. One day Marguerite gave Maeve a sketchbook and a set of pencils so she could draw. At the end of every day, as they walked back to the estate, she would critique Maeve's attempts and offer advice on how to improve her drawings. Maeve hadn't drawn since before Jeremy had been born and it felt such a relief to be able to take it up again.

Maeve found her fascinating, although a little frighten-ing. But the walks back to the estate in the evenings, when Marguerite would open Maeve's sketchbook and pronounce on what she'd done, were so important to Maeve that she can still remember, almost word for word, what the painter said.

No perspective, Marguerite said tersely of a meadow sketch. *No feeling,* she said of a drawing of a tree. *No sur-prises,* she said about a portrait of herself. Sometimes she would stop suddenly and Maeve would bang into her with the wheelbarrow from behind. *Look at this,* she would say, pointing in the sketchbook to the stem of a flower or the rise of a hill. *That has movement. That sings.* She was not one to give praise easily, and those moments when she found something to extol in one of the drawings would carry Maeve through the rest of the day. The morning when Marguerite left, at the end of the summer, Maeve went into her room and wept right through the afternoon.

The church basement bomb shelter is damp and smells of wet stone. There are wooden benches set along the walls. When Harriet sits down on one she realizes that it is an old pew. People sit facing the opposite bench, as though they are travelling in a train carriage. There is an oil lamp in the centre of the floor and a couple of people have electric torches, but the lighting is too dim for Harriet to have a good look at the room. Opposite her is a woman with two small children, one nestled under each arm. The mother bows her head to one and then the other, never looking up.

There are roughly fifteen people in the bomb shelter, four to a bench. The corners of the room are in shadow so Harriet can't be sure that the flaps of black she sees there are people or the dark tuck of the stone walls.

There's a hollow booming sound above them, and the basement shudders. Harriet is exhausted, feels she can't endure another blast. Her nerves are completely raw.

"I wanted to enlist," explains Jeremy. "I wanted to fight the Jerries, but they won't let me."

"Why not?"

"I'm colour-blind."

Harriet turns on the bench and looks at Jeremy as though she will be able to tell from staring into his eyes what they are capable of seeing. He has dark hair, eyebrows that are two black slashes across his face, lips that are pale. He appears older than he had on the roof of the cathedral.

"You don't see red or green?" she asks because she knows that, like dogs, certain people can't make out all the colours in the spectrum.

"I don't see any colour," says Jeremy. "It's a severe sort of colour-blindness."

"You only see in black and white?"

"Well." Jeremy grins at her and Harriet can't help but smile back. "I don't think of it as black and white. It's more like night and day." He looks around the small underground room. "That wall opposite is night. That lamp is day. His hair is night. You." He smiles at Harriet again. "You are a sunny day."

"Flatterer," says Harriet, but she is secretly pleased.

A man passes silently along the pews with a tin cup and bucket of water. Harriet and Jeremy take a drink. The water is soft and cool and tastes of stone.

On the bench beside Harriet are an elderly man and woman. The woman sits bolt upright, her hands curled around each other in her lap. The man has removed his hat. This is, after all, a church. They stare straight ahead, as

68

though they are on a journey, are watching the countryside unfold before them.

We could die here, thinks Harriet. And worse, we are prepared for it.

Jeremy shifts on the bench, shifts again. "My mother will be worried about me," he says. "There's just the two of us. She relies on me."

Harriet's own mother never did a thing for her. A good thing. She sent Harriet out to root the potatoes, collect the eggs, bring in the coal. Once, she showed her daughter how to press flowers but later, in a fit of rage, she crumbled the dry, delicate blossoms into the fire. Harriet can't imagine that her mother ever worried about her. She eventually went mad, trying to burn the house down with Harriet inside.

Harriet crosses her legs, uncrosses them on the hard wooden pew. Her mother remains a mystery to her, a woman full of alarming volatility. She always said she was full of passion, but Harriet now thinks she was just full of rage. When Harriet was brave enough to move away with Owen, her mother did burn the house down, with herself inside it.

For a long time Harriet thought it was her fault, and then one day she didn't, and that felt worse because at least when it was her fault her guilt kept her tied to her mother. Being absolved freed her not just of responsibility but of connection. For a long time she had lain awake, imagining her childhood home ablaze, her mother's screaming face at an upstairs window. The last time she made a visit to her father, at the start of this war, he was drunk for the entire three days she was there. He couldn't drive her to the station to catch her train home because he had passed out in the potting shed. She had to walk, and then, because she was in danger of missing her train, she had to cadge a lift with the milkman.

"Do you have any family waiting for you?" asks Jeremy.

"No. I'm alone."

One of the children opposite Harriet has begun to cry. Small, ratcheting sobs break from her body until the room and the dark are filled with the noise of her crying. Harriet wants her to stop, wants her to shut up.

"I'm unbelievably selfish," she says to Jeremy, but he appears not to have heard her.

"I work at the Triumph plant," he says. "I'm training to be a motor mechanic."

At a time when the rest of the country faces massive unemployment, there is work to be found in vehicle production at Coventry. There are factories for the production of automobiles, Lancaster bombers, and tanks.

"It's what they're coming for, isn't it?" says Harriet. "All the factories. It's why we're being bombed."

The crying child will not shut up. The sobs are more frantic, quicker.

"You make it sound as though it's my fault," says Jeremy.

"I didn't mean to."

And then Harriet knows why the crying child is fraying her nerves. The noise of the sobs, their rhythm, reminds her of the ack-ack guns the Coventry defence is using tonight against the German bombers. Harriet can't abide the noise of the guns, is glad she hasn't been able to hear them over the noise of the bombing raid. The guns make her think of Owen, dying in that muddy field in Belgium.

Harriet can't bear to think of Owen. "Tell me about your job," she says to Jeremy.

"I'm apprenticing. And we only moved here this summer, before the raids started, so I haven't been at it long."

"Tell me anyway," says Harriet.

Jeremy stretches his legs out. He has long legs, like Owen.

"I'm learning about engines," he says. "I'm learning how things work."

"What do you like about it?"

Jeremy hesitates for a moment. "I like to think that an engine is a system, like a heart. The hoses are veins; the oil is blood. The engine valves are the valves of a heart, opening and closing, producing energy for the engine to run."

"What don't you like about it?"

"I don't know."

"There must be something," says Harriet impatiently. The child's cries seem to be increasing in volume with each breath it takes.

"I suppose," says Jeremy, "what I don't like is that the moment you fix something, it starts to break down again, that an engine works against itself. By its very act of running, it weakens itself, tries to come undone. Everything is slowly worked loose by the vibrations of the moving engine."

Just like us, thinks Harriet.

Underneath the child's crying there is a new sound, the low keen of someone moaning. Harriet can't tell who is moaning, but it sounds as if it's coming from the dark fold in the far corner of the room. Farther away, muffled, but still distinct, are the thuds of the bombs landing, the crash of buildings falling.

I can't stand this, she thinks, we could be buried alive, and when Jeremy says, "What?" she realizes that she has said it out loud.

―――――――――

It amazes Harriet that she stayed in Coventry; though it wasn't so much that she has stayed as that there never seemed a good time to leave. At first she couldn't go because it was the last place she'd been with Owen. It had been their first place together—the small flat on Berkeley Road—and how could she leave those last traces of him that rivered through those rooms? Then she'd stayed for his family, but she and Owen hadn't been married long enough for her to have become close to his parents, and after a few years they seemed to forget all about her. But by this time she had the job at the coal merchant's and a routine to her days that brought her comfort. She bicycled to work, walked out to the shops at lunch, cooked herself an egg for dinner or a bit of mackerel or some potted meat on toast. And by this time she had begun her discovery of Coventry, had started to research the history and explore the city and surrounding countryside. She had become attached to a place where she'd never imagined living by imagining life there before her.

At the library she discovered that Coventry was once part of a Roman road that went from Leicester to Mancetter. She spent a day walking up and down the old Roman riverbed of what had become Cox Street and wrote her description of it that evening.

> *Water running underground sounds like a woman crying. People often mistake streams beneath their houses for ghosts. The land on which St. John's Church is built is right where a lake used to be and the church is prone to flooding. There is a word I remember from my childhood—guzzle—a low, perhaps damp spot on an estuary or inland from a beach, as far inland sometimes as to be a field, where the sea can enter if it chooses. It is a place that is really a ghost, because it exists only under certain conditions, when water remembers where it has gone and what it has touched; when it imagines*

what shape it once filled and held. When it remembers
who it used to be.

———————

There is a sudden crash and clatter, and a large metal object, smoke and dust spilling from it, skids to a stop at the bottom of the stone stairs.

"It's a bomb," cries one of the men. "Don't move." And then, realizing as everyone in the shelter is realizing, that it is an unexploded bomb, he yells, "Get out. Get out before it goes off."

"Don't panic," says Jeremy to Harriet and then to the roomful of people.

The bomb blocks the section of floor in front of the basement steps. The cylinder has been dented by the tumble down the church stairs. Harriet can see the crumple of metal in the muted light of the oil lamp and thinks she can hear a hissing coming from the interior of the bomb. She stands up slowly and treads carefully, pressing herself against the damp stone wall of the basement in order to get past it.

She is one of the first to get out, to emerge into the cacophony of the city, which suddenly seems, absurdly, like a safe place. Jeremy is right behind her, and behind him follows the rest of the group. There is no explosion. The bomb must be defective or has simply refused to detonate on impact. No matter, everyone who was in the church basement disperses.

In the shelter, they were in it together. In the chaos of the bombed city, they return to being strangers.

For a moment Harriet thinks that Jeremy will leave, will scatter with the others, but he stays with her. And then she remembers that he doesn't know how to find his way through the city without her.

The air is so filled with dust it is hard to breathe. Harriet inhales and chokes. She can smell something strange, the odour of cooked meat. It is the smell of roasted pork. There must be a butcher shop burning nearby.

Barrage balloons, huge and whalelike, are tethered just above the remaining roofs of the buildings. She hears the clang of fire engine bells but no engines. They must be stuck behind the rubble that is starting to crowd the streets.

Wires are down and flames leap like dancers in the empty window frames of bombed shops. A river of fire runs down the street.

"Look out!" yells a man near Harriet. "It's from the dairy."

Harriet realizes that it's a slick stream of burning butter. To her left is a crater with a double-decker bus in it.

"Stay away from the buildings," says Harriet. She has to yell to be heard above the noise of the bombing. "Stay with me."

They need to get out of the middle of Coventry. They have a better chance of survival on the smaller streets, the ones farther away from the centre of the city. Harriet reaches for Jeremy's hand and they run, lungs full of smoke and dust, lungs full of the dead air of the city, down the middle of Bayley Street.

The bombing shakes the ground so that the people fleeing through the streets stumble as though drunk. The trembling earth shifts them one way, and then another, and Harriet finds herself reaching out to steady herself on walls that are no longer standing. She falls in the street, picks herself up from the shaking ground, and falls again. Her leg is bruised. The combination of debris, noise, and the shaking ground makes her lose her bearings. The hot waves of air pull her hair straight back, push the air out of her lungs.

She tightens her grip on Jeremy's hand. We are the lucky ones, she thinks. The ones who have escaped. The unlucky ones were sheltering under their furniture, or crouched in their cellars, when the whole house dropped to its knees, drowning them in bricks and beams, burying them under everything they once held dear.

The singing has subsided and a melancholy gloom has descended over the inhabitants of the bomb cellar in The Coachman. Maeve prefers the melancholy to the singing. At least it's quieter. She is worrying about Jeremy as she listens to the rhythm of the bombs falling overhead, trying to decide if there has been any break in the action.

"Sounds like it's intensifying," says the publican, and Maeve has to agree that it is getting worse.

They have been instructed by the government to seek shelter during an air raid, but there has never been any mention of what to do if the air raid doesn't end. What if the city is destroyed? Is it the best choice to remain entombed in the basement of a pub? Maeve's house is literally around the corner. Surely she has a good chance of getting back there, and once she is there she can shelter under her massive oak dining table. Perhaps Jeremy has returned to the house while she's been in the pub basement.

She stands up.

"What are you doing?" says the sparrow man.

"I'm leaving."

"You can't do that. It's too dangerous."

"I live close by, and I need to get back home to my son," says Maeve.

"I can't let you go," says the publican. "We need to stay in the cellar until the all-clear."

"Are you going to stop me?" asks Maeve.

There is a silence, and in the silence, while the publican ponders whether he should physically restrain her, Maeve nimbly steps over the people in her way and bolts up the cellar staircase.

The pub is as it was when they left it to stumble down the cellar stairs. The tables still hold the pint glasses, each one containing its measure of beer. The fire still burns, casting wires of light out into the room. The front window is still intact. Everything looks the same, but when Maeve passes the table where she had been sitting, she puts a hand down on the wood, and when she lifts it up it is covered in dust. She briefly considers finishing her pint, but the dust dissuades her from this.

Outside, the world blooms and fades, flaring bright and then subsiding. The ground trembles and the noise of the exploding bombs is deep and guttural, something felt as well as heard, something that resounds through Maeve's body like a heartbeat. There is the cough of the ack-ack guns and the drone of the bombers. They're flying so low over the city that when Maeve looks up she can actually see, in one bomber, the outline of the German pilot in the cockpit.

The street is still passable. Only one house is down, on the corner, and the debris is confined to the radius of the building. But beyond, toward the centre of the city where Jeremy is, things must be much worse.

What seems strange to Maeve is not the downed house but the deserted street. She has never been on it when it has been empty of people and traffic. Maeve runs down the centre of the street. She gets to the corner, tries not to look at the destroyed house because she is afraid of seeing a body, and turns onto her street.

Nothing has been hit. All of the houses are intact. Maeve

runs the rest of the way home, pushing open the iron gate and racing up the path to the front door. It is absurd to think that Jeremy would have been able to make it back from the middle of town so quickly, but she barges into the house calling his name and rushing up the stairs to check his room.

He is not there. She sits down on his sloppily made bed. The room is mostly in darkness, but the moon outside the window lights the row of tin soldiers that Jeremy keeps on his window ledge. He saved up his pocket money to buy them when he was a boy. They are turned to face one another, rifles raised, bayonets attached. There's a Gatling gun in the midst of them that shoots real matchsticks. For the first time, Maeve realizes that the tin soldiers are modelled on soldiers in the last war. They are Jeremy's last station of childhood, and the sight of their frozen combat unnerves her. She turns her attention to her son's bed, pulling the sheets tight, plumping the pillow, smoothing the eiderdown. The pillow still holds the shape of Jeremy's sleeping head.

Maeve had gone to a good school. She was expected to go on to university and, if not that, at least to marry well. She was the only child of older, wealthy parents, and there was a lot of expectation placed upon her.

She had done nothing of what her parents had wanted and very little of what she herself had wanted. But she knows that she has been happy. Her life has been perfect. Even on the bad days there is always something to cleave to, something small, the way the leaves show their undersides in the rain or the way the rain falls in great veils, sweeping down from the darkened sky.

Of course, a great deal of the reason for her happiness has been Jeremy. Every time she looked at him he just seemed so solidly good. She was always glad to see him, always interested in his news, always hopeful for his future.

Maeve sits down on the neatly made bed. She thinks of all the places she and Jeremy have been. What their life has consisted of. There was the pub where she was a barmaid. The Bucket of Blood, so named because it had once been an abattoir. The low stone building still had the stench of death about it. Maeve would sometimes wake in the night and swear she could hear the bellow of cattle, could feel their fear rising up through the floorboards of her bedroom.

At the plant nursery, where she went next, Maeve and Jeremy lived in a hired caravan in the field just behind the nursery. The caravan had a musty smell that never went away, no matter how often Maeve hung out the bedding in the sun or scrubbed down the wooden walls of the interior. They had to cook over an open fire outside, and Maeve mostly didn't bother. They ate cold food, and once a week she would take Jeremy to a pub for a hot evening meal. That was the only time they were ever warm, those Friday evenings at the pub.

The caravan ran with damp. They had to sleep in a tangled knot in the centre of the bed or else the water running down the walls would soak the bedding. Field mice regularly made nests in their stored clothes and chewed through the tea towels. Once, they came home to find a badger sitting calmly on the caravan steps as though he lived there.

The field they walked through to get from the nursery to the caravan was muddy, full of furrows, and Maeve was forever scraping the thick clods of mud from the soles of their shoes. Water for washing had to be hauled from the nursery, and so they washed less than they should. Jeremy looked feral after a couple of months in the caravan.

It was better at work than it was at rest. At the nursery, Maeve liked walking between the potted roses, inhaling their scent. She liked the sway of the saplings in the breeze. She liked the way everything flowered, on time, even though nothing was planted in the earth.

The next job Maeve took was as a dressmaker's assistant. At the dressmaker's, part of the work was to make the customers feel good about the dresses they were having fitted. Most of this involved lying. Maeve would stand to one side, with pins bristling out of her sleeves for pinning up the hem of the dress being fitted, and she would have to flatter the woman who was buying it. *That colour looks so lovely on you,* she would say, when in truth the woman was a hog and had chosen fabric that was the exact colour of hog skin.

But Maeve remembers the dusty light of the shop at the end of the day when she locked up. She remembers the dresses, half made, holding the evening light inside them, like lanterns, as she pulled the door of the shop closed and looked back at them through the window. They always seemed more beautiful empty than they did when they were filled with a human form, and this was the sad truth she wished she could tell the customers but was never brave enough to do so.

What kind of life had she given Jeremy? What kind of life had she given herself? If they survive this night, she will never move again.

———————

Harriet and Jeremy see the horses on High Street. Three horses running down the road, their manes lifting through the smoke, their hooves knocking on the cobblestones. Three night horses. The horses run right past them, close enough to touch. They are running away from the fire and the bombing, running toward the open fan of countryside outside of the city.

Above them, Harriet can hear the bombers. The planes come in waves and sound exactly like that, like the pulse and pound of sea on the sand, a muffled, rhythmic heaviness. She doesn't look up, even though, on such a clear night she might be able to make out the shape of the planes. But they have been warned not to watch bombing raids, not to gaze upward, as the pilots might see the reflection of their faces in the light of the fires and use their faces as guides to drop their bombs.

The horses are gone now, disappearing into the smoke and the dust, into the frantic darkness. Perhaps their stable burned down and they escaped; or perhaps the horses were set free by their owner. On their own they have a better chance of surviving. Their flight is swifter than human flight. Their instincts are sharper.

The Old Palace Yard, where Harriet has sometimes come to concerts with Wendell Mumby, is a heap of rubble. She remembers the untidy Tudor beauty of the building, how the upper storey leant out over the lower storey, how the panes in the upper storey windows shivered with age. It was a building full of sombre wood and streaky light. Harriet remembers the smooth feel of the stair railing, how it slid under her hand as she ascended to the second floor.

"Look," cries Jeremy. He seems to be less afraid now, to have taken on new energy.

There are two men stumbling along in front of them. Each holds on to an end of a door. Lying on the door is a woman. Her clothes are torn and her head is twisted unnaturally on her body. They disappear into the smoke up ahead.

Now that Harriet has seen one body she suddenly begins to notice that all around them are the dead and injured. In their flight down High Street they pass the bodies of dead men and women, limbs visible, soft shapes beneath the hard shift of the collapsed buildings. They see a child's body lying in the road, thrown there by the blast of a bomb. Even though she has lived through the other, earlier raids, Harriet can see that this one is much worse. She never saw bodies before. Those raids were over quickly, leaving their targets destroyed but much else intact. This raid seems intent on destroying everything.

At one point Harriet hears an ambulance siren, but never sees the actual vehicle. The rescue services don't seem to be able to push through the wreckage.

"This is worse than the other raids," yells Jeremy, echoing her thoughts.

The farther they stumble through the centre of the city, the more Harriet understands how catastrophic is the damage. Buses are on their sides. The tramlines are ripped up, the steel rails twisted as easily as the wire of a coat hanger.

Harriet's mother used to recite something about the trams. Harriet remembers how it frightened her when she was young, the sight of her mother's face leering over her bed in the dark.

Mama, Mama, what is that mess
That looks like strawberry jam?
Hush, hush, my dear, 'tis just Papa,
Run over by a tram.

Is she losing her mind?

"Over here," yells Jeremy. He's kneeling down beside a pile of bricks. Harriet hears the high-pitched whine of a bomb falling, cringes and covers her head, but the bomb explodes a few streets over. She coughs from the dust, scrambles over to Jeremy, who is frantically digging through the bricks. "I saw his hand move," he says, and Harriet looks down and sees a man's hand, palm open to the night, and the rest of the man covered in debris.

She gets down on her hands and knees and begins pulling rubble off his body.

He's a man not much older than Harriet, but by the time they get him free, he's dead.

"Look at that," says Jeremy, pointing to the medals that the man wears pinned to his chest, perhaps in an effort to save them. "Mons. Ypres. The Somme. He went through all that and he died like this."

Harriet thinks of the medals she was given after Owen died; the medals he had earned but never received. It felt, at the time, as though she was being awarded the medals for sacrificing her husband to the war. She gave the metal stars and ribbons to Owen's parents.

A man emerges from a lane supporting another man. "Help me," he says when he sees Harriet and Jeremy. "I can't carry him much farther."

Jeremy rushes forward and hoists the injured man up against his shoulder.

"Where can we take him?" asks Harriet. She is sure the hospital has been flattened by now.

"I don't know," says the able-bodied man. "But I can't leave him. He's my friend."

The injured man appears to be unconscious, his head is slung down against his chest. Dragging him through the streets will make them more vulnerable to being hit. Harriet doesn't want to risk her own life to save a stranger's. She knows this is selfish, but she doesn't care.

The two men carrying the door appear again. This time there is a young girl lying on the wooden stretcher. What happened to the first woman? Harriet rushes back to her little group.

"Hurry up," she says. "We need to follow those men with the door."

The would-be ambulance attendants do not go far. As they disappear down a passage at the end of a row of shops, Harriet follows them. At the back of the shops, sitting on the bare patch of land beyond the dustbins, is an Anderson shelter with perhaps half a dozen people sitting or lying on the ground in front of it. The men with the girl on the door tip her off onto a bit of clear ground and then shuffle back up the passage.

Harriet runs back to the others.

"It's a bomb shelter," she says to Jeremy. "Just behind the shops. Looks as if it's been turned into a kind of aid station."

The Anderson shelters have been given out by the government to anyone in Coventry who has wanted one. They are made of curved pieces of corrugated sheet metal that bolt together and are meant to protect against flying debris but they are not sturdy enough to survive a direct hit.

A young woman strides out of the shelter. She has her hair tied up in a kerchief and a first-aider's satchel slung across her shoulder. She looks up at Harriet and Jeremy, at the man Jeremy is helping to drag toward the shelter.

"Oh, god," she says. "Not another one. All right. Lay him down. Make sure he's breathing. Keep him comfortable. I'll get to him when I can." She kneels by the girl who has just been dumped off the door, looks up at Jeremy and Harriet in their fire-watcher uniforms. "Could you help me carry her inside? I'm all by myself here."

"Sorry." The man who is helping Jeremy to carry the injured man untangles himself from his burden. "I left my family. I need to be getting back to them," and he grimaces apologetically as he scuttles off.

"Of course we'll help you," says Jeremy. He gently lowers the injured man to the ground, lays him on his back, and takes off his own coat to use as a pillow under the man's head.

"Are you a doctor?" asks Harriet.

"Nurse," says the woman. She stands up, offers her hand, first to Jeremy and then to Harriet. "Marjorie Hatton. I was taking shelter here and a bomb fell on those shops. Some people managed to drag themselves out and I salvaged some of the bolts of fabric for bandages." She waves her hand toward the length of cloth wound tight around a man's chest. "Chintz," she says. "Not sure he's going to think much of those pink flowers when he wakes up."

Harriet is always suspicious of people who seem unnaturally cheerful.

Another wave of bombers passes overhead and Marjorie Hatton ducks through the doorway of the shelter.

"We can't stay here," says Harriet. "What about your mother?" She doesn't want to go inside the shelter. She doesn't want to help the wounded. She can't explain this to Jeremy without sounding cruel. She has had enough of death. One of the injured reaches out in his pain and delirium and grabs hold of her ankle. She has to shake hard to dislodge him.

"My mother can take care of herself," says Jeremy. "She's good at that. It's me she'll be worried about." He moves to follow Marjorie into the shelter, looks back at Harriet. "And you don't need to stay here on account of me." He leaves her standing alone. Harriet follows Marjorie and Jeremy into the bomb shelter. She is annoyed that Jeremy could so easily dispense with her.

Inside, two lanterns hang from the ceiling, illuminating the makeshift hospital. On each of the two benches set along the side walls of the shelter are two patients, stretched out, covered in blankets, one patient quiet and one moaning and moving her head about. On the dirt floor of the shelter are bolts of fabric and several saucepans of water. It is impossible to stand up straight, and even in the few moments she has been inside the shelter, Harriet feels that she's getting the beginnings of a migraine from stooping over.

"Here," says Marjorie, leading them to the woman who is tossing her head from side to side. "She's cut her leg badly and needs stitching. I need one of you to help hold her down while I sew her up."

Jeremy immediately moves forward to help. He avoids looking at Harriet, and she can't tell if he cares or not that she came after him. She can't bear to think of sewing up the young girl's leg without anaesthetic. I'm selfish, she thinks. I'm selfish and inflexible and so used to being alone that I no longer know how to relate to people. But she is still hurt. She has brought him this far through the burning city. She feels responsible for him.

Marjorie is trying to thread a needle by the dim light of one of the lanterns. "God," she says. "What I wouldn't give for a cup of tea."

"I'll go," says Harriet. "I'll go and get you one."

"Don't be mad," says Jeremy. "You'll be blown to bits out there."

"No," says Harriet, "I can see it's what's needed. Tea. I'll go and get you a cup." And before Jeremy can say anything more, she backs out of the shelter. It was a noble gesture, but now that she is back outside again, she has no idea where in hell she will be able to find anything that resembles tea. If the water mains have been hit, then there will be no such thing as hot water. There will be no boiling a kettle, even if she manages to find one.

She creeps along the back of the shops instead of returning to the main street. There's a crater where the last shop in the row used to stand. She can see the tatters of dark cloth waving about inside, like streamers from the deck of an ocean liner. It looks blue in the moonlight. Coventry blue. The cloth made in Coventry was once prized for the lasting qualities of its blue dye.

Harriet kicks at a brick in her path. She can feel the smouldering heat of it through her shoe. But there seems to be a lull in the bombing.

She passes half a house, the front half—the back half is blown off. In the maze of charred beams a man is wearing a bowl on his head and is standing in front of a broken mirror. He is stripped to the waist and holds a razor. A steady stream of water drips from over his head, from the open floor above his head, into another bowl set on a strip of wood before him. He dips the razor into the bowl, raises it to his face. He is shaving.

He waves at Harriet when he sees her. "Have to keep up my good looks," he says. "Might be back at work tomorrow."

Harriet looks at the stream of water falling from above. "Is that hot water?" she asks.

"It is indeed. The bomb heated up my rainwater tank. It's

as hot as though it came fresh from the boiler. That's why I'm shaving now."

"Do you think I might borrow some to make tea?"

"Help yourself." The man waves his razor toward the wreck of his house. "I'm afraid my crockery is crocked, and I don't know where the tea has got to, but you're welcome to the water."

Harriet is cheered by finding what surely must be the most elusive component in the tea-making process. "Thank you," she says. "I'll be back." She moves a few feet on, stops, cocks her head to one side. She can hear something else. "What's that ringing?" she asks.

"Doorbell," says the man. "The bomb gave me hot water and it also burned through the wires, fused my front and back doorbells permanently on. And," he says, dipping his razor back into the bowl of water, "it destroyed pretty well everything in my house, except for the half-dozen eggs I bought yesterday, and of those not a one is broken." He shakes his head. "What madness. You're welcome to have an egg with your tea if you like."

"I'll be back," says Harriet again, and she continues her slow walk over the bomb debris.

She finds a pot standing upright on a pile of bricks as though it had just been placed there by an unseen hand. The lid is missing and there is a dent on one side, but it's fit enough to make tea in.

The air is smoky, but the moon is so bright that it is easy to see where she is going. Harriet moves slowly on. She wishes she hadn't been so snide to the nurse at the shelter.

The bombing starts up again. Harriet crouches on the ground, puts her arms up to cover her head. The ground shakes and there is dust in her eyes and mouth. Something glances off her arm and she feels the sting on her skin that means she has been scraped to bleeding. She reaches up and puts the saucepan she's holding on her head. It fits her better than the fire-watcher's helmet did.

Ahead not a building is standing. She will have to go back.

The shaving man is gone, along with what was left of his house. Harriet wades through the wreckage. Water is still dripping from the ceiling. She puts up her hand and feels the heat of it slide through her fingers, rubs her hand across her eyes. The man is lying under a wooden beam. At first she can't see him, he is so covered in debris. His eyes are staring open, but his chest has been crushed in. Harriet pushes aside bits of wood, twisted pieces of metal, the shattered mirror; tugs at his arm, but she can't get him out. He's wedged in too securely. She reaches down and touches his cheek, still warm and smooth from shaving, then she looks to see if he still holds the razor in his hands. His fist is closed around something. She kicks through more wood to clear some space, and then she kneels down, uncurls the dead man's fingers, and finds the twist of tea cupped securely in the palm of his hand.

She crouches beside him for a moment. His kindness has touched her, and she doesn't want to leave him alone. But it is foolishness to remain out in the open, keeping the dead company. Harriet pockets the twist of tea, puts her hand up to the dead man's face, and gently closes his eyes.

———————

There was a day a few years ago, a cold day, when the wind snapped in the trees, and Harriet walked out with a cloud of breath slung above her. She wandered over the snowy fields outside Coventry, following the weave of old stone walls across the landscape. She was trying to write a description of the walls, had become obsessed with them, how they were made by human effort though they looked so natural. Harriet remembers that day as joyful, a rarity in her days. Somehow the walking and the cold and the weave of the walls and her foggy breath pulled her back to early childhood, to a feeling of being wholly present and wholly purposeful.

The stone walls are scattered like broken, human music across the countryside. Used to mark boundaries, they were made from clearing the fields. The size of the stones gets progressively smaller as the walls get higher. The large stones are all at the base of the wall, and the walls themselves are only as high as my waist. Perhaps this is as high as a man can lift a stone without strain. Perhaps this is as high as a man can lift a stone without having to raise his hands above his heart.

The walls are like language. They are like fine tracery with the light behind them, like lace, and, in a sense, they are no different from these words—each one lifted slowly into place and balanced on this page.

———————

Coventry was once a walled city, and two city gates survive, with a piece of wall running between them. Harriet stood for an hour in a garden one summer, where there was still a good section of the wall intact. The people who lived in the house had trained fruit trees to grow up the wall, their branches creeping tentatively out among the stones, like fingers reaching for a hold on a rocky climb. Harriet ate a pear and tried to count the stones, lost count, standing in the sunny garden with the sweet taste of pear filling her open mouth.

The walls would be of no help now, thinks Harriet, approaching the door of the Anderson shelter. Who could have imagined that the attack that would bring down Coventry, all these years later, would be coming from above? It is always the thing that you can't imagine that is your downfall, she thinks, pushing open the door and stepping into the warm darkness of the shelter. Because the thing you can't imagine happening is what you can't ever guard against.

"Oh, Harriet," says Jeremy, and she can tell from his voice, from the relief in his voice, that he is glad to see her back.

She holds out the saucepan triumphantly toward him. "Tea," she says. "No milk, I'm afraid, and we'll all have to drink from the one pot—but it is hot enough, and it is tea."

"You're a marvel," says Marjorie. She takes a sip of the tea, bends to offer the pot to the girl who has just been stitched up.

Jeremy takes a sip from the saucepan of tea when it is handed off to him. "That was a bit mad," he says. He reaches out and touches Harriet on the arm. "You've cut yourself."

"I was caught in a blast." Harriet looks down and sees that her forearm is slippery with blood.

"Sit down," says Jeremy. "I'll wrap it up for you." He leads her to a bench and she dutifully sits down, holding her arm out before her for him to bandage.

"What colour does it look like to you?" she asks.

"What?" says Jeremy.

"The blood."

"Darkness."

But this isn't right. Harriet thinks of the salty taste of blood, the slickness of it, and the heat. How it is protected inside the wall of your body, and how when that wall of flesh is breached, it rivers out, moves along a course of its own choosing. She thinks of the bloody chest of the dead man.

"Blood isn't darkness," she says. Blood is the fruit of darkness.

Jeremy is quiet for a moment, and then he leans down and kisses Harriet's arm; his lips touch her blood.

"Yes," he says, "I can see what you mean."

————————

Maeve tries to imagine Jeremy safely tucked away in a bomb shelter. She tries to imagine that he is not afraid, that he is not alone. But thoughts of him sitting calmly underground, chatting to the other inhabitants of the shelter, quickly turn into memories of him as a child, terrified and crying. Her memory of him moves swiftly from childhood to manhood and back again.

Maeve stands up, runs her hands over the eiderdown to smooth it, and then goes downstairs. She should eat something, but she's not hungry. She should crawl under her dining table to shelter, but she's too restless to settle.

She stands at the window in the sitting room, watching the flashes of light in the sky above the garden. For the first time she wishes that she knew who Jeremy's father was so there would be someone to share her worry, someone to stand beside her here at the window and reassure her.

Jeremy's father was one of several soldiers in the last war.

Maeve had not had what one could call a proper relationship with any of them. They were soldiers on leave when she had met them, and she was swayed by the intensity of their feelings for her—feelings she realizes now were motivated by their fear that they would die shortly on the battlefield. She had not loved them, but she had believed that each one of them had loved her, and she felt tenderness toward them because of this.

Now she barely remembers their names.

Whenever Jeremy asked about his father, Maeve simply said he had been a soldier who had died in the last war. She has no idea what happened to those men she bedded with such sweet urgency, but all of them could well have been killed.

Maeve has never really been in love. She has waited for a relationship, but it has simply never happened. The fact of her son keeps most men away, and the ones who do come near want sex. Maeve is always insulted by the assumption that just because she has had a child out of wedlock, she is easily persuaded to bed.

Maeve has never questioned her life. Things happened or didn't happen. She didn't care about the reasons. But now, standing here, she wishes she'd known Jeremy's father, that she'd married him, that they'd made a home together. Yet she knows that that wouldn't have necessarily kept Jeremy safe. Having another person to love, having a family, would just mean that she would have more to lose on this terrible night.

―――――

"I want to go home now," Harriet says to Jeremy. "I don't have much, but I want to see if it's still there. I want to make sure Wendell Mumby is safe. Besides, I don't want to die in an Anderson shelter."

Jeremy has finished wrapping her arm in the piece of chintz, tied a neat knot just below her elbow to hold the fabric in place. "I'll come with you," he says. He seems more fond of her since she returned from her quest for tea.

When they tell Marjorie Hatton that they must be off, she thanks them and shakes their hands solemnly, as she did when she first met them. The gesture seems both formal and intimate, as is everything to do with the war, everything that is happening to Harriet on this night.

"It's not going to stop," says Jeremy when they step out the shelter door and see the surge of fire on the horizon. "It's not going to stop until there's nothing left."

They head back down the passage to High Street.

"Let's go through the park," says Harriet. "It's quicker." She leads the way. The streets are more deserted now. Harriet is amazed at how quickly she has become used to seeing dead bodies. We must be in shock, she thinks. All of us, all of Coventry. We must all be in shock.

There is an explosion near enough to them so that the wall of heat from the blast slams against them and knocks

them flat. They lie there, Jeremy half on top of Harriet, pro-
tecting her with his body.

Harriet's ears ring from the blast. She's lying face down
in the road. She can taste the damp stone, and her eyes water
from the grit and dust.

Jeremy is lying with his chest across her back, and even
though she is afraid, his weight is comforting. When the air
has settled and he scrambles up, Harriet misses the feeling
of his body lying across hers.

The water mains have been hit. The electrical supply is
knocked out. The phone lines are down. The buildings that
haven't collapsed have their windows gone. Blackout curtains
hang in rags from the window frames. The buildings that
have suffered direct hits release debris into the air—bricks
and bits of wood, slate tiles, a glittering crescendo of window
glass. Harriet and Jeremy run through the streets with their
arms covering their heads to ward off the wreckage.

In the park there are incendiaries standing upright in the
grass, like candles. There are a couple of fire-watchers in hel-
mets trying to put them out, kicking them over and stamping on them. By the time Jeremy and Harriet stumble over
to help, the incendiaries have been extinguished. It is still
impossible to talk without shouting. It is easier not to talk,
and they weave across the grass in silence.

The leaves have burned black on the trees. The limbs are
twisted and full of clothes, caught there like strange birds in

the upper branches. The clothes must have blown up there from a bomb blast.

Harriet remembers the morning of November 14. How beautiful it was, all sun, and only a little wind to remind her of autumn. It was early closing. It was a Thursday. She had gone round to the shops before lunch, and she had felt lucky because she was first in line at the butcher and got sausages.

———————

Maeve walks through her darkened house. She drags her fingers along the walls, feeling the nicks and bumps in the wallpaper that she didn't know were there. The house isn't familiar enough to her yet to allow her to walk around freely with the lights off. She needs to touch the walls for guidance.

The texture of the wallpaper feels like the sand on the beach where Maeve remembers having a picnic once, between the wars. She was with a man she barely knew, and she was waiting for him to kiss her while Jeremy raced behind them, in and out of the surf. She had been dragging her hand back and forth through the sand beside her while she waited for this man, whose name she has forgotten, to get up enough courage to lean across the picnic blanket toward her.

Maeve stops by the kitchen door. The house shakes from a nearby blast and she puts both hands out to steady herself against the door frame.

It was a perfect day, she thinks, that day at the seaside. There was sun and good food, the tension of waiting to be kissed, the happiness of watching Jeremy running through the waves. What she had felt was not the usual hurry to be on to the next moment but a desire to linger where she was.

Maeve wouldn't have minded dying then, when she was happy like that—except for Jeremy. But not now, she thinks, pushing off from the kitchen doorway and drifting back into the hallway. Please, not now.

———

Harriet and Jeremy are nearing the end of the park. They have come more than half a mile perhaps and are nearly home. Remarkably few trees are down or on fire. It seems, except for the heavy thud of the bombs falling around them and the smoky light rising over the city, almost normal.

"What's that?" shouts Jeremy, pointing to a misty shape by a thicket of bushes.

At first Harriet thinks it's a trick of the light, but the shape moves its head and she can see that it is a horse. A white horse, head down, feeding on the grass. Maybe it is one of the horses that passed us in the street, she thinks. They instinctively move toward it, walking slowly over the grass to where it stands, oblivious.

"Look there," says Jeremy in Harriet's ear. "To the right of the horse, by that tree. Isn't that a person?"

A woman sits up against the tree, her head slouched forward against her chest. She has long blonde hair, with patches of dark that Harriet can see, once they get closer, are blood. She wears clothes that suggest she was on her way home from the office—a skirt and blouse. A cardigan lies beside her on the grass, and her shoes are gone. One of her legs is bent unnaturally back.

"It's broken," says Jeremy as they get closer.

The horse, now sensing them, throws its head back and whinnies. The woman jerks upright at the sound. Harriet and Jeremy kneel down on either side of her.

"I think I'm seeing things," whispers the woman. "I think there's something wrong with my eyes."

They crouch down beside her. Now that they're close to her, Harriet can see how matted with blood the woman's hair is.

"It's a horse," says Jeremy. "You're not seeing things."

"How did you get here?" asks Harriet.

"Dragged myself," says the woman. She shakes her head and blood splatters across Jeremy's face. "I'm dizzy," she says. "Can't seem to clear my head. And cold." Harriet puts a hand out and touches the woman's skin. It's colder than the air around them.

"She's freezing," she says to Jeremy. They both move closer to the woman, trying to warm her with the heat of their bodies.

"I don't think we should move her," says Jeremy. "I don't think we could get her back to Marjorie's." He doesn't say the words *in time,* but Harriet knows what he means.

"Is it really a horse?" says the woman.

"I think so," says Harriet, but she's not sure about anything any more. The horse could be a mirage. It seems a ghostly apparition, and the way it is calmly feeding seems out of step with the panic of the evening.

"How strange," says the woman. Her head lolls to one side and she slips down in one movement onto Jeremy's lap. He cradles her head in his arms, looks up at Harriet.

"What do I do?" he asks.

"I think you're doing it," says Harriet.

It takes a long time for the woman to die. Her breath becomes ragged, and then it bubbles in her throat and Harriet thinks she is dead, but the breathing starts up again, and then stalls, goes quiet. They sit holding her until she grows completely still. It is suddenly quiet in the park, a pause between the waves of bombers overhead.

They pick up the woman as gently as they can. Jeremy carries her by the shoulders, and Harriet lifts up the woman's feet. The weight of the dead woman is the same weight as the sacks of coal she would sometimes help move out of the storage room at work. They stagger over to the small copse of trees just behind them, lay her down on some soft grass. Harriet folds the woman's arms across her chest.

"We should say something," says Jeremy, but they stand there, beside the dead woman, and there seems nothing they can say. For all her descriptions, for all her careful search and rescue of words, Harriet can think of nothing that would equal this moment. No half-forgotten prayer from childhood. No lines of poetry.

When they come out of the trees the horse is gone. They walk over to the spot where it had stood. There is nothing to show that it was ever there—no indentations in the grass.

Harriet reaches up and wipes blood from Jeremy's face with her sleeve.

And in that moment, they hear the same distant familiar sound, hear it again, and turn to each other for corroboration. It is the bells of the cathedral, sounding the midnight hour.

———————

Maeve remembers lying in her bed as a child and listening to the birds outside her window. She remembers the patch of light on the wall opposite, how it changed shape as the sun moved up in the sky. When she first woke it was a triangle, and when she actually got out of bed it had stretched out to a rectangle.

She remembers the bitter taste of gooseberries, and how she used to stand behind the gooseberry bush at the bottom of the garden, hidden from the house, and cram her mouth full of the fruit, never sure if she would have to spit them out because the taste was so sharp. She remembers the shape of the dog's paw when it was sleeping, how the paw bent backwards and each of the pads was a delicate black oval. She remembers the smooth of the ivy leaves that grew up the stone wall of the house and how, at the end of the day, they were warm from the sun when she put her face to them.

This was my time here on earth, she thinks, and suddenly it seems to have been full of the most amazing things.

Maeve comes out of the sitting room to find the next-door neighbours in her front hall.

"We saw you running down the road," says Agnes. "And we wondered if you'd be wanting to come with us."

"Where are you going?"

"We're evacuating," says Richard. "Going out into the countryside. It will be safer there."

"Everyone will be leaving," says Agnes. "The bombing's not letting up. The city will be flattened by morning."

"But my son isn't back yet," says Maeve. "I have to wait for him."

"Won't he be evacuating as well?" asks Richard. "Won't you have a better chance at being reunited with him outside the city?"

There have been other moments in Maeve's life when she's had to make a definitive choice. When she found out she was pregnant she had to decide whether to give the baby up. When various suitors had proposed marriage, she had to decide whether she wanted them, or simply the easier life they offered. When she felt restless with a situation or a place, she had to decide whether to stay put or go elsewhere.

Maeve recognizes this moment at the bottom of the staircase as being one of those times when she must make a choice between two unknowns. What is the best thing to do? If she remains here, the house could be bombed and she could be killed before Jeremy returns. Or he could come back within the hour. If she evacuates into the countryside, she could meet her son there or she could never find him again.

The dark pocket at the bottom of the stairs holds the three figures, motionless and shadowy.

When the choice was whether to move on or stay put, Maeve always chose to move on. When the choice was to join up with someone or remain alone, Maeve chose the latter. When the choice was to keep her illegitimate child or give him up for adoption, Maeve chose to keep him. Given her nature and her experience, the odds are even as to whether she will go with Richard and Agnes or stay waiting.

Maeve had been thinking of giving Jeremy up after she gave birth to him. It was the easier thing to do. Her family would welcome her back, indeed they would pretend that the whole unpleasant business had never happened. But when Maeve was handed the baby, when she saw him for the first time, she felt the string connecting them. Whenever Jeremy moved or cried, Maeve felt tugged toward him. It didn't feel like a choice to keep him. It felt as though it was the only thing she could do.

If Maeve stays in the house, her life is more at risk than if she walks out of Coventry. She is no good to her son dead or injured.

She closes her eyes. She can see the tiny creature Jeremy once was. She can still feel the tug between his needs and her actions. He is alive, she knows that. And he is a sensible boy. He likes systems and plans, the logical approach. If he is safe, he will stay put until the bombing is over. If he is in danger, he is more likely to find his way to safety than to remain at risk.

Maeve opens her eyes. Behind the grey figures of Richard and Agnes she can see the glow of the moon over the smoky garden. When Jeremy was born, there was a moon as bright as this one. She remembers it shining through the window at the end of the ward. She took its brightness to be a good omen.

"I'll come with you," she says. "Just let me go and fetch my coat."

Maeve hastily puts on her coat and scarf. She writes a note for Jeremy and leaves it on the kitchen table. She jams an apple and a torch into one pocket, her sketchbook and pencil into the other. She can't think of what else to take, and so she doesn't take anything, just follows Richard and Agnes out onto the street.

They hurry up the road, turn the corner, and head away from the city. Almost immediately they see other people, other travellers through the darkness. Some people are pushing prams or wheelbarrows loaded with belongings. Some people are carrying children. One old man leads a donkey.

It makes Maeve ill to think she is leaving Jeremy in Coventry, so she tries to think instead that she is going toward him, that he's waiting for her in the countryside. She falls into step beside Richard and the man with the donkey, and she imagines Jeremy walking this same road, just ahead of her, just in front, barely out of sight.

―――――――

The library has been bombed. Most of it is burning. Harriet can feel the heat from the flames trickle across her skin. She and Jeremy are crouched behind a wall of rubble across the street from the fire. The library burning is worse for Harriet than the cathedral burning. The reference room had these lovely stone arches and open shelves, two floors high. Harriet used to stand on the balcony, looking down over the railing at the long wooden tables with the uncomfortable chairs, at the men and women, heads bowed solemnly over their books.

When a building is lost, everything that had happened within its walls is lost as well.

Jeremy's head is close to Harriet's. She can feel his breath on her cheek. She wants to know if the world in which she lives, this place where she is using herself up every day, will remember anything of her. Will the buildings that she has carefully studied, walked through, touched—will they recall her footsteps, the weight of her body on the stone steps, the smooth flat of her hand on the banister? Will the cobble-stones hold her footfall? Will the river or the rain remember the shape of her body?

Harriet is sure she can smell the books burning in the library. She thinks she can smell the pages turning to ash, all the pages she has pored through, the paper thick and slightly damp, the edges of the pages brown with foxing and sometimes sticky to the touch. She used to pride herself on all the information she knew. For some reason it was a comfort, all this knowledge she could unravel with a breath. Now, that still contemplation she had in the library seems completely unreal.

Maybe reading was just a way to make her feel less alone, to keep her company. When you read something you are stopped, the moment is stayed, you can sometimes be there more fully than you can in your real life.

A bomb falls nearby and they duck down farther behind the wall. Jeremy holds his hands over Harriet's head, as if he is holding an umbrella for her, as if what falls is simply rain.

Harriet closes her eyes. She can feel the heat from the burning library against her eyelids. She remembers an old book on colour that showed a patch of colour, and then it linked that colour to places in nature where it was found. Everything was described in the most delicate way. A white was described as *the white of the human eyeball* or *the inside quill feathers of the kittiwake.* It was the reference book that Charles Darwin took with him on the *Beagle* when he went to South America. It was how he identified and catalogued the creatures he saw there. She remembers taking the heavy book down from the shelf, opening it on the library table. The colour patches still seemed brilliant. The descriptions were written in spidery handwriting. Sometimes there were blanks, as there was no vegetable to match *the breast of a lapwing,* no mineral that could be linked to the *scarlet leadington apple.* Harriet liked to try to fill in these blank spots, to match up a colour with the colour on a bird's wing, or a mouse's belly, or a stone pulled from a riverbed.

> *How would I describe the world? By describing something, doesn't the thing itself cease to exist? How would I decide what to marry—this shade of grey with the low-slung clouds of November. Not precise enough. This shade of grey is cigarette ash. That shade of grey is water running over clay. Not vivid enough. That shade of grey is old mortar between old bricks.*

Jeremy is quiet beside her. Harriet puts a hand on his arm. He had rolled up his sleeve when he was working in the aid shelter. His skin is soft under her fingertips, softer than her own.

"We should go," she says.

Harriet and Jeremy move away from the library, continue on down Hertford Street. Home is not far now. From inside some of the shops there is a sound like artillery fire. It takes a while to determine that it is the noise not of gunfire but of the tinned goods in the shops exploding. They pass a row of houses burned to nothing but their frames, and yet on the windowsill of each house is a cat, curled up, nose to tail.

Cats stay with the building, thinks Harriet. Dogs go with the people. They have seen many dogs scuttling along the streets, pressed tight against the walls, tails between their legs, or nosing through the rubble, looking for their owners. Jeremy has put his hand out to several of the dogs, but they are too skittish to come near. But the cats seem relaxed, sitting in their places like sentinels.

The route they are travelling means that they will get to Harriet's house before Jeremy's. Harriet wishes she had taken them another way, but the other ways were blocked. She doesn't feel ready to arrive at her house yet. She feels better able to deal with Jeremy's impending grief rather than her own. She has less to lose.

A bomb explodes a little way in front of them. Harriet can feel the blast of hot air push her backwards. She puts her hands over her head to protect herself.

The bombs falling on the city are an unnatural phenom-
enon, and yet they have to be thought of through past experience. The people of Coventry have lived through storms.
They have listened to the bass notes of bells, and so the
bombs become all of these things. The bombs feel to Harriet
like an earthquake shaking the ground, lightning striking the
earth, the deep, sonorous toll of a bell.

When something is unnatural, there is no new language
for it. The words to describe it must be borrowed words, from
the old language of natural things.

This must be how it was for Owen, thinks Harriet. This
never knowing what will happen next, this living in constant
peril. She is worn down by one night of it. She can't imagine how Owen must have felt after days and days of living
like this. Maybe he wasn't killed in the trenches but crawling
away from there. One of the customers of Bartlett's Coal had
fought in Ypres. He had told Harriet once that the ground
near the trenches was packed with so many bodies that it was
as springy as a mattress.

A few years after Harriet had gone to Ypres, the town
was rebuilt. A memorial was constructed at the Menin Gate.
Harriet saw photographs of the rebuilt church, the buildings
in the centre of the town repaired and looking as though
they'd never been bombed. It was a shame, she thought, that
they'd seen fit to do that. Not that she couldn't understand

the need of the people who lived there to go on with their lives, to have back what had been taken from them; but she had thought that the ruined town was a much better memorial to the dead than the rebuilt one. There was a dignity and a sorrow in the desecrated buildings that wasn't present in the redone models. They spoke more directly to what had happened there. There was more truth in them.

What will happen to Coventry? she thinks. Will there be anything left to rebuild, to memorialize? It is so hard to tell how much of the city has been destroyed, how great the damage is. But so much seems to be gone, and the bombers just keep coming back. There will be nothing left by morning. And what of the next night? The Germans could keep it up until everything and everyone is extinguished.

"Let's go," yells Jeremy into her ear, and she realizes that the bombing has moved off, moved away from them. She stands up stiffly, her arm aching, struggles through the rubble.

The smoke-shrouded moon shines high above them now, straight overhead. The sky is as red as blood.

They reach the end of Berkeley Road without incident, and then it happens, the moment that Harriet has been dreading. They turn the corner and begin to move down toward her house. They hurry past where Mrs. Patterson's house used to stand, just a crater there now. The rose hedge that used to front the garden has been completely buried in rubble. The house next door to Mrs. Patterson's is standing, and the one next to that.

"Which one's yours?" shouts Jeremy.

"At the end of that row." Harriet can't look for fear of what she might see. She looks down at the ground instead, at her feet moving carefully around the bricks and bits of broken wood. "Look for me," she says to Jeremy. "It's the last house in the row. Mine was the flat on the top floor. Wendell Mumby lived below me."

"It's gone," Jeremy says. "The last half of the terrace is gone."

Harriet looks up then and sees immediately that there is nothing left of her house, or the one beside it, or the one beside that one. The wall still surrounds the garden, but the garden is entirely gone.

"Wendell," she says. Jeremy has his arm around Harriet's shoulders and she leans into the hollow of his collarbone. Jeremy smells of smoke and camphor. His skin is gritty against Harriet's face.

She is afraid that she will find the body of Wendell Mumby in the rubble, but if he is there, he is well buried under the bricks and broken pieces of furniture. Her flat has collapsed into the ground-floor flat. Even so, she finds precious little that has remained intact.

"Look for my wedding photograph," she tells Jeremy. "It's in a silver frame."

They are moving cautiously over the debris. Even with the bright of the moon it is still hard to see properly.

"You're married?" says Jeremy.

"Was married. My husband died in the last war."

In the photograph, Harriet and Owen are standing at the door of the church. She has the bottom of her dress gathered in her hand because they're about to go down the stone steps. Owen is wearing a morning coat. The photograph has stood on Harriet's bedside table since he died. Every night she goes to sleep looking at it, and every morning she wakes up doing the same.

They don't find the photograph. All they find is a small wooden box covered with shells that Harriet had kept buttons in. The buttons are gone, but the box has remained whole. They find pages of books and fragments of crockery. Jeremy unearths a bent spoon, straightens it, and hands it to Harriet. Not knowing what to do with it, she puts it in the box covered in shells.

"Mrs. Marsh," calls a voice, and Harriet looks down from the hill of rubble to see her neighbour Mr. Carter from the other end of the terrace.

"Have you seen Mr. Mumby?" shouts Harriet.

Mr. Carter shakes his head. "No," he says. "But I have your cat. I have Abigail."

———————

The Carters' house is as it ever was, not even a window blown out. It seems miraculous to walk inside and see all the cups and saucers intact, sitting on the shelves the way they always have.

There's a hurricane lamp on the worktop, and candles burning for light. Mrs. Carter pours them water from a large saucepan on the floor. "You're welcome to shelter here with us until morning," she says.

The elderly Carters and their equally elderly collie, Jack, have been lying on a mattress under their heavy oak dining table for protection against the bombs.

"The cat won't come near the dog," says Mr. Carter, leading them into the kitchen. "She prefers the upstairs landing window. We found her sitting on the wall of your garden."

Harriet leaves Jeremy in the kitchen with Mr. and Mrs. Carter and bolts the stairs two at a time. Abigail, just as reported, is curled up on the ledge of the window at the top of the stairs. She meows when she sees Harriet, and Harriet bursts into tears. It is not that she is overly fond of the cat. She was a stray that Harriet took in and initially they merely tolerated each other. But Harriet has grown attached to her and now, except for that vulgar box coated in shells, she is the only thing she has left. She reaches out her hand and strokes the cat's head, rubbing behind her ears as Abigail likes. When she takes her hand away, it is dusty with ash.

"What happened to Wendell?" Harriet asks Abigail.

"Where did he go?" Abigail meows again, and then gets down to the serious business of grooming her right back leg.

Jeremy is crouched under the table with the Carter family. The plates rattle on the shelves as a bomb explodes nearby. The dog appears to be asleep.

"He's deaf, poor lamb," says Mrs. Carter.

"Lucky dog," says Jeremy.

The dog kicks out his legs in his sleep, dreaming of running.

"No sign of Wendell?" Harriet asks.

"We haven't see him," says Mrs. Carter.

Another bomb goes off. Chunks of plaster fall from the ceiling onto the table. Everyone flinches, even though they're not hit.

"I can't believe my house is gone," Harriet says to Jeremy. She keeps alternately forgetting and remembering this fact. She feels disembodied.

"Poor lamb," says Mrs. Carter, patting Harriet's knee.

They're close together under the table. Harriet has to keep shifting on the mattress to avoid coming into contact with Mrs. Carter or Jeremy. Mr. Carter keeps patting her shoulder. She is getting a cramp in her calf from the unnatural way her legs are bent. Her arm aches and her throat is sore. Wendell is gone. Her house is destroyed. The cat is safe. This is the sum total of her life.

"I should go to my house," whispers Jeremy in her ear. "I need to find my mother."

Harriet feels immense relief when he says this. She found the Carters boring before the war, and even though she is grateful for their kindness, she is eager to get away from their well-meaning blandness.

———————

The donkey's name is Amos. He is not impressed with the bombing, or with the long night perambulation he is being forced to undertake. Periodically he stops dead in the road and the man leading him has to lean his weight backwards on the rope to get Amos moving again.

Maeve likes the irritable donkey, his stubborn refusal to do as he is bidden. She likes the undulations of his leg and shoulder muscles as he walks. She likes the smooth grey wall of him, less than an arm's length away from her own body. She looks at him as much as possible, trying to memorize him so that she'll be able to draw him later on.

No one talks. The line of evacuees just moves forward, each step taking them farther away from Coventry, farther away from this terrible night of destruction and death.

Maeve eats her apple and gives half to the donkey. His teeth are big and yellow; even in the moonlit darkness she can see their tarnish. He must be an old donkey. He takes the piece of apple from the flat of Maeve's hand and stops to eat, chewing with his mouth open, as all animals do.

Jeremy would have liked Amos, thinks Maeve, and then she reprimands herself for using the past tense to think about her son. Jeremy *will* like Amos.

When Maeve first came to Coventry five months ago, she had a little money saved from her last job and didn't have to work right away. She put her energy into setting up the house and getting Jeremy settled into his job at Triumph. She was waiting to hear if she'd been accepted to work as a post-man; with so many men away they were taking women. But this hadn't happened yet. She spent her days looking after domestic duties and then, in the afternoons, she worked on her drawing. Not since she was a young girl had she had such a calm routine. This autumn had been almost a rest because the pace of her days had been so relaxed.

Maeve thinks of this now, as she's walking along the road, the city slowly dimming behind her. She has been happy with the rhythm of her days. It is not as though she's greedy for happiness, but she wishes that she'd been able to recognize it completely when she had it.

Maeve remembers the light in the front room in the afternoon, how it crawled from the settee to the sideboard to the fireplace mantel. She remembers the creak on the stair-case when Jeremy thudded down in the morning, the slower creaking as he ascended at night. She remembers the clink of milk bottles on the stone steps, the sputter of sausages under the grill. There was always a breeze in the garden when she was hanging out the wash. It filled the sheets as though they were sails.

These were ordinary moments. They were not filled with meaning, but they were Maeve's life. Nothing that will come after tonight will be her known world. If she and Jeremy survive tonight, there will be the struggle of beginning again. This is hard enough at the best of times, but in the middle of a war it will be almost impossible to bear.

Maeve wipes the tears away that have started down her cheeks. She has slowed without realizing it, and is no longer keeping pace with Richard or the donkey. She has fallen behind. She is alone among this moving wall of strangers.

————————

Harriet and Jeremy pass the fallen house of Mrs. Patterson and turn the corner. Harriet feels enormous relief at leaving her wrecked house behind. Wendell Mumby is buried under the rubble of it. It has become his grave. The invincibility she felt earlier in the evening seems to have evaporated. She thinks it is likely that Jeremy's mother is dead too, and that she and Jeremy could be killed before the night is over. They are foolish to be out on the streets of Coventry when almost everyone else is hiding from the bombs. But when they were in that church basement earlier, Harriet had felt claustrophobic, and surely the cellars will be like ovens, with the city on fire above them. It feels better to be above ground, to be moving about, to see what is happening, rather than just imagining it. It would be better to die outside than trapped in a cellar with people she doesn't like or know.

Jeremy's street is perhaps five minutes away. Harriet does not know what will happen when they reach his house. If the house has survived, and he finds his mother, what will become of Harriet? Will he simply thank her for being his guide and expect her to disappear back into the night?

Harriet never wanted that much from her life, and what she did get was taken away. What will happen to her after this? Will she have to go back down south, throw herself on the mercy of her remaining relatives? She has been wilfully bad about keeping in touch with any of her family. She's not even sure where anyone is except for her drunken father. Surely she won't have to go and live with him again. How could she bear that?

Harriet looks over at Jeremy, walking beside her. She barely knows him, and yet he seems known to her. She likes his long limbs and the way, even when he's hurrying out of danger, he ambles along. It's reassuring to her. Harriet has not been in such accordance with anyone for as long as she can remember. An affinity, that's what it is, she thinks. She feels an affinity with young Jeremy Fisher, and she badly wants to keep it.

There has been a pause in the bombing. Maybe it is over at last.

Harriet realizes that Jeremy has been speaking and she hasn't been listening.

"What?" she says.

"I liked this place," says Jeremy. "I thought we'd stay here. I liked my job at Triumph, and the house was close by, and Mum was looking into getting a job as a postman." Women were now filling a lot of the traditionally male positions. One of the women Harriet used to work with at the coal merchants had left to become a welder because the pay was better and she fancied herself a sort of dragon, spraying fire over great sheets of steel. *Everyone would have to stay out of my way* is how she'd described it to Harriet.

They turn onto Jeremy's street.

"Where are you?" asks Harriet.

"In the middle there, on the left."

Mayfield has sustained much less damage than Berkeley. There don't seem to be any houses down, just a few windows blown out and pieces of rubble scattered about the street, probably lifted there from bombs that have exploded nearby.

Jeremy's house is standing. There is a window gone

downstairs, and a door from some other house lying in the front garden. Harriet feels a wave of envy.

"You're a lucky man," she says, but Jeremy isn't listening, is no longer standing beside her. He has bolted up the path, pushing open the front door, which swings easily off the latch.

"Mum," he bellows into the interior of the house. "Mummy."

The inside of the house is not in as good condition as the outside. The kitchen is a mess of smashed china. There are balls rolling around on the floor. It takes Harriet a while to get her eyes accustomed to the darkness in the kitchen and realize that the balls are really potatoes. There are bits of glass from the smashed front window in the sitting room. The hanging lamp in the front hall has come away from the plaster ceiling.

Jeremy has gone upstairs and Harriet follows him. She meets him on the landing. The finial on the stair rail comes off in her hand when she grabs it to steady herself.

"She's not here," says Jeremy. "No sign of her. I can't tell how long she's been gone."

"She probably went to a shelter."

"Or she wasn't at home when the air raid started." Jeremy drops down to sit on the top step. "She likes to go to the pub in the evening, to have a drink and draw in her sketchbook. I left home at four and she was here then, but she could have gone after that."

"She's probably safe," says Harriet, thinking of Wendell Mumby, who is probably not safe, is probably squashed flat under the pile of rubble that their shared home has become.

"But what now?" says Jeremy. "Do I keep looking for her? Do I stay here?" The building shakes from a nearby bomb blast and plaster dust falls from the ceiling like flour sifting down. The raid is certainly nowhere near over. If anything, the frequency of the bombing has increased in the last little while.

"Stay here," says Harriet. She only knows that she doesn't want Jeremy to leave her. "We could stay here until morning, and then we could do a proper search for your mother. It will be hard to find her in the dark if we don't know where to look."

Harriet drops down beside him on the stairs. Their legs are touching.

Jeremy cocks his head to one side and looks at her. "All right," he says. "We'll stay."

In the silence Harriet can hear the trickling of plaster down the wall behind them.

"Would you like something to eat?" says Jeremy. "I'm forgetting my manners."

"No, thank you," says Harriet. She pauses. "Do you have manners?" she asks.

"I do."

"Do you have a girl?"

"No." Jeremy shifts on the staircase and moves, ever so slightly, toward Harriet. "I told myself I was in love with Lily Palmer, but she didn't love me back. She went with a pilot. I can't really compete with the RAF." He smiles.

"How old are you?" asks Harriet.

"Twenty-two."

"That's half my age, exactly."

"You don't look over forty," says Jeremy.

"You haven't seen me in daylight."

They are quiet again. Harriet feels suddenly shy.

Jeremy takes her hand. "I keep thinking of that woman in the park."

"So do I."

"Is there blood on me?" he asks.

"Up near the collar and a bit on the sleeve. Here." She moves her other hand, the one not holding his, and turns the piece of overall sleeve above his wrist so that he can see the patch of blood. They are turned toward each other now, close enough to kiss. The thought frightens her so much that she drops Jeremy's hand.

"You said the pub around the corner was where your mother went?"

"Yes."

"Let's go and look for her," says Harriet, standing up.

———

The Coachman is still standing. The front door opens to a touch. The bar is empty and the fire is out, but Harriet can see the pint glasses on the tables in the moonlight from the open door. They are covered with dust.

Jeremy finds the door to the cellar at the back of the pub and wrenches it open. They can hear voices down there, see the stuttering light from candles.

"Hello," calls Jeremy as they begin their descent. "Hello."

The cellar is small and damp. The knot of people in the centre of the room are quiet as Harriet and Jeremy come down the staircase.

"We're a bit full, mate," says one of the men, finally.

"We're not wanting to stay," says Jeremy. "I'm looking for my mother. She might have been here earlier?"

"There was a woman here when the sirens first started," says another man. "She was sitting by herself in the pub, drawing pictures."

"That's her," says Jeremy.

"Said she was going home to her son," says the man.

———————

When they get back to the house, Jeremy stands for a moment in the front hall, absorbing the stillness of the building.

"God," he says, looking down at his sleeve. "I still have that woman's blood on me. I can't stand this. I'm going to go and change." He bounds up the flight of stairs and disappears into his bedroom.

Harriet can't help following Jeremy. She doesn't want to be separated from him now. She stands in the doorway to his room, watching him unbutton his overalls. The moonlight slanting through the bedroom window makes everything look milky.

It's a boy's room, not a man's room. There is a cricket bat leaning against a wall and shelves holding toy cars, even a line of soldiers marching across the window ledge. There is a teddy bear on the bed, leaking straw through its belly.

Jeremy has unbuttoned the uniform but hasn't removed it yet. He looks over at Harriet standing in the doorway. She has to think quickly.

"What's the most precious thing you have?" she asks.

"That's worth the most?"

"That means the most."

Jeremy walks over to the window ledge and takes a small object from there, brings it over to Harriet at the doorway.

The tiny coal fire on three miniature legs glows red from some combination of paint and a sparkly stone. Perhaps mica, thinks Harriet, remembering suddenly the page of minerals in a book on geology that she once looked at in the library.

"It's supposed to warm the soldiers in the sentry box," says Jeremy. "They come together as a sort of set, the sentry box and the fire. When I was a boy I just moved my soldiers around the fire, to warm them up." He looks at the coal fire, burning in the palm of his hand. "I don't know why I like it so much," he says. "But it's sort of perfect, I think."

"It's almost like a jewel," says Harriet.

"Yes," says Jeremy. He holds it out toward Harriet. "Here," he says. "You have it."

"No, I didn't mean that," she says. "I don't want anything."

"You have it," says Jeremy. He presses it into her hand, closes her fingers over it. "So you'll remember me."

"How could I forget you?" asks Harriet.

Jeremy puts his hands gently on Harriet's shoulders. "I don't know what to do," he says. "Tell me what to do."

Harriet can feel her heart ticking in her chest. "Do what you want to do," she says.

Jeremy hesitates for only a moment, obediently struggles his arms from the sleeves of his overalls. They slide down his body, drop onto the floor.

Their embrace is awkward and desperate. They stumble onto the bed. When Jeremy kisses Harriet, he tastes of smoke. He tastes of the burning city.

Harriet's overalls are still attached by one ankle. Jeremy's socks are on, and his underpants are pulled down around his knees. The bed is narrow and Harriet's head knocks against the headboard for the few thrusts that Jeremy manages before he shudders to a stop, lying heavy and damp on top of her.

There is a moment of complete calm. A moment when Harriet can see the light changing in the bedroom window over Jeremy's shoulder. Now it looks like a saucer. Now it looks like the prow of a ship.

She runs her hands over Jeremy's back, feeling the joinery of spine, the latch of ribs. He doesn't say anything, and it takes Harriet a moment to realize that he has fallen asleep. She feels completely exhausted too, but she doesn't want to sleep through this moment.

———————

Harriet knows Jeremy is awake when she feels his body stiffen. He doesn't look at her, struggles up, off the bed. "I should go."

"No, don't go. Please."

Jeremy is hastily pulling on trousers. He walks over to the wardrobe to get a shirt. "I should go back out and help the others. I should go back out to Marjorie Hatton's aid station and help her. I'm sure my mother must be safe, wherever she is, and I'll find her here when the raid's over." He puts on a shirt, doesn't stop to button it up, bends down to tie his shoes. "Think of that poor woman in the park, and the old man buried under the rubble."

Old man. The dead man with the medals on his chest from the last war had been barely older than Harriet.

"Jeremy," she says, but he doesn't look over at her, doesn't stop to answer her. He laces his shoes and bolts from the room.

Harriet lies on the bed, listening for the sound of the front door opening and closing. The small fire, curled tight in her fingers, feels as though it is burning a hole through her skin.

She feels as though it is her fault that he has left, embarrassed at what has happened between them. She wants to run after him, make him come back to her; but Jeremy doesn't owe her anything. He's not obligated in any way. They were together this evening because they chose to be, and now he has chosen to go off alone. Harriet has to let him.

Harriet thinks of Owen, how she always saw him as a man when they were together—because she was young then too, because she looked up to him. But now she can see how he, too, was still only a boy.

————

Harriet has been out with only one other man after Owen. It was about five years ago, and it didn't last long. His name was Stanley, and he was the younger brother of one of her bosses. He had come to town for a visit and she had been invited to have dinner with the whole entourage of wives and bosses. It was a set-up; she'd known it from the start. It may even have been presented to her that way by Mr. Bartlett. *Stanley is alone, and I know you are too, Harriet.* The dinner was bearable because there were so many people there that Harriet didn't really need to talk to Stanley, but afterwards he offered to walk her home and she felt she had to oblige him. He wasn't in the coal business, which was a relief as Harriet found the coal business rather boring. Stanley had moved away from the family enterprise. He'd become a law clerk, although he seemed to fancy himself a proper barrister. They walked through the streets and he regaled Harriet with points of law that she couldn't care less about. He never asked her a single question about herself, and when they got to the wall outside her flat he pressed himself against her and pushed a hand up her skirt.

"What are you doing?" she had said, wriggling away from him.

He looked affronted at her non-cooperation. "You're a widow," he said. "It's what you want."

"It's not what I want at all," she said.

"But how can you not want a man's attentions?" asked her friend Daisy, several years after Owen's death.

Harriet couldn't explain that she didn't really feel like having a physical relationship with anyone. She felt lonely, but she blamed it on Owen dying. It was as though love and sex was a room she had once entered, and now she had simply left that room, turned off the lights, and gently closed the door. It didn't feel as though she had given up anything. It had given her up.

———————

Harriet stands in front of Jeremy's house, looking up at the window of his bedroom. She opens her hand, looks at the small soldier's fire lying there, and then tucks it into the pocket of the coat she has borrowed from a peg in the hallway and begins walking.

Harriet can't go back into the city. It makes no sense to do that. She knows how much damage is there, how hard it will be to find shelter; so she decides she will head in the other direction instead. She leaves Jeremy's street and turns toward Warwick Road, one of the main thoroughfares of Coventry that leads into the countryside. She will walk out of the city.

———————

These are the drawings that Maeve has wanted to make but hasn't been able to: the shoe that dangles from her mother's foot when she sits with her legs crossed, how provocative it seems, and how that one gesture doesn't match anything else about her character. The mother who did not accept her for who she was.

The dead hedgehog she found in the garden last week. There were no marks on its body, and it was still standing up, as if it had been walking along the ground and had simply died.

Her own face in the dressing-table mirror in her bedroom. She has actually tried to do this before, has spent a week attempting a self-portrait. Every day for a week she sat down on the stool embroidered with roses in front of her dressing table and drew lines on the page, looked up at the planes of her face, looked back down to the paper. Each self-portrait had looked nothing like the next and that had surprised Maeve. She had always thought of herself as remarkably constant. The drawing had showed her that perhaps she was adaptable, and that, when the moment changed, she was able to change with it.

Maeve stops when the donkey does. It makes sense to her that the animal will know when he's safe. She doesn't want to go too far away from Coventry in case Jeremy is still there. She sees the donkey being led into a field, and she follows it.

There is no organization. No one seems to be in charge of taking people's names or offering any sort of aid. People wander aimlessly around the dark field, too nervous and restless to settle. It's quieter and darker out in the countryside because there isn't the light from the fires. Maeve notices this right away; also colder, as there isn't the heat from the scorched and burning city to warm the night air. The bombing is muffled and distant and suddenly seems elsewhere rather than overhead.

Amos is grazing. His owner has let the rope around the donkey's neck go slack and is having a cigarette.

Maeve runs her hand over the flanks of the donkey. There are raised lines of flesh under his fur.

"Do you whip him?" she asks the owner, not able to stop herself.

"He was whipped," says the old man. "But not by me." He turns toward Maeve, the end of his cigarette burning a hole in the darkness between them. "He was my daughter's pet," he says. "When she was a little girl. She raised him. We lived on a farm then." He strokes the donkey's neck. Amos is undeterred from his task of eating the grass.

"My daughter grew up and moved away, and we sold the donkey. He changed hands a few times and I lost track of his whereabouts. Then one day I was doing some work for a farmer and I saw the donkey in his field. He had welts all over him from being beaten." The man drops his cigarette and grinds it out under his boot. "My daughter loved the animal," he says. "So I bought him back."

"Well, that's a nice thing to do," says Maeve.

"Not entirely," says the old man. "You see, it was the wrong donkey. I took it home and my wife said it wasn't the right donkey. My daughter's donkey had a white patch near one ear." The man pulls on the donkey's ear and it brays in irritation. "See, nothing."

"Yes," says Maeve, even though it's too dark to be able to notice where the white patch might have been.

The man pauses for a moment, enough time for Maeve to guess what he's going to say next. "My wife was killed, standing in the kitchen, making us a cup of tea."

The smoke from his cigarette curls up around his head like a halo. Maeve doesn't know what to say in response to his story. She looks around the field, at all the darkened figures shifting around the perimeter. Everyone in this field, everyone in the city will have been touched by the bombing raid. Everyone will have lost someone or something tonight. Everyone will have to remake their lives. And the men dropping the bombs, the men in the planes slicing through the darkness, they will bear no witness to the misery and suffering they've caused.

———

Jeremy isn't in the field. Maeve walks every inch of it, peers into every face she sees, asks everyone if they've seen her son. He isn't here, but she tells herself that this doesn't mean he won't appear. Every moment there are more people emptying out into the field. He could show up five minutes from now, an hour from now.

It is just after two in the morning. Maeve asked someone for the time, having left her watch in her house. It has been seven hours since the bombing started and there are still flashes over Coventry to indicate it is continuing unabated. Jeremy could still be sheltering in the basement of the cathedral. He might not make it out of the city until morning.

Maeve settles down against a hay bale near the road where she will have a good view of the evacuees. If her son is walking past, she will be close enough to see him. She watches the road, watches the people who leave the mass of refugees and drift into the field. She watches those who keep going. She knows Jeremy so well that she could recognize him in an instant—his profile, his walk, his clothes, the way he rubs his head sometimes when he's nervous. All she has to do is scan the crowd every few minutes. If he comes, she will not miss him.

These are the things that Maeve has drawn in the sketchbook she has with her tonight: a rabbit, an elm tree, an old barn, a shingle beach, Jeremy.

The rabbit was the one that had come near her in the field this evening. The tree was one in a long avenue of elms that she had seen last week from the window of a bus. She had bicycled back to the trees the next day to draw it, bringing her folding stool and a flask of tea. What she liked about the elms was how twisted their bare branches were, as though each tree had been grasped from above and given a half turn in the earth. The branches seemed tentacled and melancholy.

Even the bark was split and twisted, so that there wasn't a single straight line for her pencil to follow.

The barn was in the field behind her parents' house in Sussex. She had been down recently on a reluctant visit, leaving Jeremy to fend for himself for the weekend. She had been sitting in the garden in the weak autumn sun, having tea and listening to her father lecture her (again) about the wasted life she had chosen for herself. To stop herself from screaming, or even from talking back, Maeve had drawn the sweet collapse of the barn. Part of the roof had fallen in, and the timbers around the windows were swayed with the strain, but the barn was solidly holding on to the idea of itself as an upright building. The door was buckled but still inside the frame. The posts at the end of the barn were stubbornly vertical.

The drawing of the shingle beach was from that same visit. Maeve had told her father that she was on a later train, and had arrived at the station early and walked over to the beach. The tide was out and the shingle was wet and oily, tangled with seaweed and decorated with the odd jellyfish. Part of the beach had been cordoned off by barbed wire in case of invasion, but the section that was still used by the fishing fleet had been left open, and Maeve had walked along the stony ground for a while and then had parked herself by one of the fish huts in order to sketch the scene. What she liked was the look of the stones, how they rolled the eye toward the sea, how the sea pushed the stones back up onto the beach. It was a kind of violence, the way the water and rock interacted with each other. Each rock had been worn smooth by the constant tumble of the sea, but there had been no surrender. This was not a willing intimacy but a forced one.

The drawing of Jeremy was done quickly. He is in profile. He was with his mother at the pub for a drink. They were sitting by the fire because the evening had been cold, and the light from the fire threw shadows onto Jeremy's face that, when sketched in, make him look older and more miserable than he had indeed been that evening. The drawing is of the side of his face, one shoulder, and his arm raised at the elbow with a beer glass held in his hand. Maeve is not fond of the drawing. Jeremy looks too much like her father in it, and she feels that she has got the shadows in his face completely wrong. But she does like the ease with which he holds the pint glass. His hand is strong and it is wrapped around the glass confidently, fingers spread and flexed against the surface. She has thought about redoing the drawing just as that, as the image of her son's right hand gripping his glass of ale.

———————

There are hundreds of people, a slow procession of human traffic, drifting down Warwick Road like smoke. Some of them carry suitcases, some wheel prams and wheelbarrows stuffed with boxes. A woman walks by carrying a man's hat full of tinned beef. A man balancing a birdcage on the handlebars of his bicycle passes Harriet. She joins the line, stepping in behind a woman who holds the hands of two young children, one on either side of her.

"Where are you going?" Harriet asks the woman next to her who's pushing a pram loaded with clothes and books.

"Out," says the woman. "I'll walk to Birmingham if I have to, but I won't go back." She gestures to the pram full of belongings. "This is all I have left, and some of it is damaged."

"I have nothing either," says Harriet. "My cat survived, but I left her with my neighbours."

The woman nods in sympathy and Harriet can't think of what to say next. She misses Jeremy already, and she feels badly about how they parted. They walk in silence for a while. Harriet bows her head and concentrates on following the hem of the coat of the woman in front of her.

Jeremy could be all the way back to Marjorie Hatton's by now. Or he could be sheltering somewhere. Or he could be dead. Harriet wishes she could have him back. What if something happens to him? It will be her fault.

Instead of the wall circling the interior of Coventry, there are now just roads that lead out from the centre, like spokes in a wheel. They exit the city where the original gates for the walled city used to stand. The city gradually begins to fall away. There are trees and grasses along the road the evacuees are travelling on. In the starry distance Harriet can see the dark slant of the fields.

"What's your name?" asks the woman walking beside her.

"Harriet."

"Do you think you could have a go, Harriet? My arms are tired." The woman drops her hands from the pram, and Harriet obediently steps in to push.

"What do you have in here, rocks?" The pram springs are flattened out and the body seems to be grinding against the wheels.

"Tins," says the woman, looking suspiciously right and left, as though expecting people to jump out of the hedgerow, leap upon her, and steal her hoard of sardines or snook.

I suppose, thinks Harriet, straining against the handle of the pram, that the choice is always between sentimentality and practicality. A photograph or a tin of ham? The family silver or pots to use for carrying water?

"Do you think the bombing will last all night?" asks Harriet.

"How should I know?" says the woman.

The war has not improved people's tempers. All this talk of how it brings out the best in people is simply rubbish, thinks Harriet. Miserable people are made more miserable by the war's deprivations and dangers. Happy people can still return to being relatively cheerful. But everyone, regardless of temperament, is weary of the fighting, and nervous that they are losing the war. The fall of Coventry will be a big victory for the Germans. If Coventry could be bombed to pieces, then why not London? Surely that is how it will go, that is what will happen next.

The night is darker away from the fires of the city, away from the moon's reflection off the buildings. It is easier to talk, the farther they get from Coventry, and Harriet can hear conversations start all around her, like small fires catching on a roofline.

People gradually leave the procession. When they reach the first set of fields, many walk out of line to sleep in the grass. Harriet can understand how people are weary, but it still seems too close to the city for safety. She keeps going. Just past the first fields she passes the pram over to another willing helper.

It feels good to walk without debris underfoot, to take a long stride down the centre of the road. She feels as though she could walk forever, that she might very well continue on to Birmingham. And then, the moment she thinks this, she suddenly feels incredibly tired, as if she could collapse on the road and sleep for a year. She looks over at the man who has replaced her pushing the pram, wishing that she could scoop out the contents and curl up inside it herself.

She drops out at the second set of fields, and no one says a word when she leaves the group. The grass is wet. She can feel it whisper against her ankles as she walks into the field.

The dew is coming up. It seems bizarre that life will continue as usual, regardless of the destruction of Coventry.

All throughout the field are the forms of people sleeping in the grass, covered by coats and blankets. Some people are leaning up against the hay stooks, talking and smoking; a few people are walking slowly about the field, looking for friends and relatives perhaps.

Harriet stands near the edge of the field, looking for somewhere to lie down. It is cold away from the bombing, and she is glad that she'd had the presence of mind to borrow a coat from Jeremy's house. She wraps her arms around herself, tips her head back to the heavens. The sky is still dark, too early for there to be any sunlight leaking in at the edges. She sees the rattle of stars overhead, the first stars that have been visible all evening. The bombing continues, a soft *thud thud* over the distant city.

Harriet sits on the ground, her arms still tight around herself. She is dizzy with tiredness, but she finds it too cold to sleep, too cold even to sit for long on the grass; so she gets up again and starts walking through the field. Perhaps someone has made a small fire that she can warm herself by. Perhaps someone will be kind enough to share a blanket. She wishes that she'd had the nerve to pinch something from the woman with the pram.

She closes her eyes and then wakes, shaking off the cold, and dozes again, dreaming of Jeremy.

When she wakes, the field of people seems the dream. Harriet is reminded of a Russian novel she recently read. If this were a Russian novel, she thinks, there would be a horse in the field and an argument. There would be several loaves of bread and a long declaration of love.

She thinks this, and then she sees a horse grazing quietly a few yards away from her. She moves closer, sees that it is a donkey, not a horse, but she is still unnerved by the sight of it. The good thing about books is that they remain themselves. What happens in their pages stays there. Harriet does not like the idea of the story bleeding through into real life. She trusts a story, and doesn't trust real life. But what makes her trust a story is the knowledge that it will stay where it is, that she can visit it but that there is no chance it will visit her.

Harriet feels like a sentry, patrolling the field. She feels like one of Jeremy's soldiers, walking stiffly up and down the window ledge in his bedroom. She looks around for fire. Suddenly she sees the glow of something on the far side of a haystack. It seems mad to have spent the whole night avoiding fire, only to be seeking it out now, but Harriet is too cold to dwell on irony. She strides toward the haystack.

But it's not a fire, it's a woman with a torch. She is wrapped in a coat and scarf, leaning up against the haystack, shining her torch down on the book that lies open on her knees. She startles when Harriet rushes toward her.

"Watch it," she says. "You've made me drop my pencil."

Harriet looks down at the book again and sees that it isn't a book with words. It's a sketchbook. As the woman turns the torch about, looking for the dropped pencil, Harriet can make out the drawing of a rabbit.

She picks up the pencil from the grass by her left shoe and hands it over to the woman.

"Sit down," says Maeve. "You're swaying on your feet."

Harriet drops down beside the woman. "Did you lose your house?"

"My son. He was fire-watching tonight, like you." Maeve recognizes the uniform Harriet wears under her coat.

All around them in the field is the flare of other conversations. Sparks drift over the grass toward them. Maeve hears the words *surrender* and *headless*.

"I'd already lost everything in the last war, when my husband died," says Harriet. "And I thought there wasn't anything left for me to lose in this one. But I was wrong."

Harriet tilts her head back to the stars. There's a sharpness to the light. The stars look as though they have been nailed fast to the heavens. It was impossible to see any stars in the burning city. There was too much smoke. She can still feel the softness of Jeremy's skin when she ran her hands over his back. She can taste his mouth.

Maeve thinks that Harriet might be crying, and she raises her torch to see if this is true and sees instead the brown wool jacket she left hanging in the front hall of her house.

"I think you're wearing my coat," she says. "How can that be?"

"Your son gave it to me," says Harriet.

———————

Maeve has sat in this field for hours, waiting for Jeremy to appear. But now this strange woman has shown up, knowing her son. After they exchange names, and Harriet tells her story of struggling with Jeremy through the city, Maeve isn't so prepared to sit still and wait for morning.

"Would you draw me a map so I can find my way to the aid station?" she says to Harriet.

"The city is burning," says Harriet. "You can't go back there."

"I did the safe thing once," says Maeve. "And it was a mistake." Maeve thrusts her sketchbook toward Harriet. "Please."

"I really don't think I could," says Harriet. "So many of the places along the way will be destroyed by now." She can feel the worry from Maeve, buzzing like an electrical current from her skin. "I can't draw you a map," she says. "But I could take you there."

———————

"Are the fires still bad?" asks Harriet of a man jostling past them.

"Hasn't let up for a moment," he says. "You won't want to be going back to the city just yet."

But Maeve feels relieved to be doing something. She feels relieved to be moving again, to be going back toward where she knows Jeremy has so recently been.

"You didn't have to come with me," she says to Harriet. "I don't want to put you in any danger. I'll be all right on my own."

"You wouldn't know where to go," says Harriet. She mumbles something.

"What?"

"And I wouldn't know what to do otherwise."

The line of evacuees starts to thin as they near the city, and the people coming along the road from Coventry look blank and sombre. Many walk with their heads down. Some are crying. The road ahead is straight and level, but it feels as though Maeve and Harriet are descending into the city.

"It will be much worse than it was when you left," warns Harriet.

"I don't care," says Maeve. She would crawl through the broken city if it meant that she might find Jeremy.

In front of Maeve is a landscape of toppled buildings and mountains of rubble. Smoke and dust rise from the streets and she finds it difficult to breathe, her eyes start to run from the stinking, acrid air. It is far worse than she had imagined. Nothing looks familiar to her.

There is still the roar of planes in the sky above them. A

bomb explodes nearby. There is a blast of heat, and a spray of debris rains down. They drop behind a broken wall.

"Put your hands over your head," yells Harriet, and Maeve does as she's told. Something hot hits her knuckles and slides off. A chunk of rock smacks against the outside of the wall and rolls into the street. She thinks she can hear someone crying, but when the bits of exploding building have stopped pelting down, she doesn't hear it any more.

"Let's wait here for a moment," shouts Harriet.

The building across the road from them suddenly shivers down like water. There were probably people in there, thinks Harriet.

Maeve has rushed across the street to check for survivors in the collapsed house. *There won't be any,* Harriet wants to shout, but she follows Maeve. The naked body of a man lies tangled in the rubble. The clothes have been burned off his body. There are just strips of cloth around his wrists from the cuffs of the shirt he'd been wearing.

Before Harriet can stop her, Maeve runs to the house next door. It's still standing, but the front door has been blown off its hinges.

Inside are a man and woman sitting at a table, and underneath the table a boy plays with a wooden train. Maeve feels such relief she rushes toward them. The faces of the couple at the table are stopped. The boy under the table is frozen, his hand holding onto the front carriage of his train. They're all dead.

"Bomb blast," says Harriet in Maeve's ear. "It burns the air to nothing. The force of it must have collapsed their lungs."

Maeve allows herself to be led out of the room. "The boy," she says to Harriet when they're in the hall.

Harriet steers Maeve out of the house. "We'll find him," she says.

———————

"We went through the park," says Harriet. "Here, through this gate." She pulls Maeve into the park. There are more trees down in the park, and fewer people. There is no one stamping out incendiaries as there had been earlier. The extinguished flares lie in the grass like used firecrackers.

The clothes are still in the trees, webbed between the branches. The clothes make Maeve think that everything is underwater, that they are walking on the bottom of a riverbed. These clothes have been borne along by a swift current, and then have snagged here, on these branches.

It is quieter in the park, thinks Harriet, and then she realizes that it is quieter altogether.

"We found a horse in here," she says. "And a woman who was dying."

Maeve is reliving Jeremy's night. It is like one of those kaleidoscopes she used to have as a child. She would hold it up to her eye and turn the tube just a fraction of an inch, and the glass pieces would shift and form a completely different image.

"The horse was white," says Harriet. She looks over to the little copse of trees where the woman's body is likely still lying. How long ago that seems now.

"How old was your husband when he died?" asks Maeve.

"Eighteen."

"And how old were you?"

"The same."

It is definitely quieter. They seem to be speaking without raising their voices. Harriet turns to Maeve near a splintered tree, its branches torn off and hanging from the trunk by thin hinges of wood. There is the smell of new, green wood as they walk past it.

"I didn't do a good job of forgetting him," she says.

Maeve has known other women such as Harriet Marsh, women who have suffered a loss in the last war and never properly recovered from it. "You shouldn't blame yourself," she says.

"I'm not blaming myself," says Harriet. "Not for that anyway." They cross the last bit of grass, walk out of the park.

"It's not far," says Harriet. "I'm recognizing more than I thought I would." Much is as it was when she and Jeremy struggled through the city. She leads them carefully down another street. There is so much debris everywhere, great piles of bricks and wood, broken bits of furniture. Fires burn in the spaces between buildings. Maeve looks down at the dark of Harriet's shoes, just slightly ahead of her, and she concentrates on that, on following the curve of Harriet's heel, as she leads them back to Jeremy.

As they are walking past a mound of wreckage that used to be a house, Harriet hears the muffled screams of a woman or child coming from underneath the pile of bricks.

"Can you hear that?" she says to Maeve. They stop by the smoking ruin.

"Yes."

"Here, do you think?" Harriet starts to climb up the pile. Maeve stays on the street.

The screams sound again.

"No, over there." Maeve points to the left of Harriet and begins to clamber up the wreckage herself.

"Where are you?" yells Harriet, but there is no response. The sound of the screams is lifting up, out of the wreckage, but her own cries aren't managing to crawl down through the debris. Voices, like heat, rise to fill the space above them.

"Tell us where you are," yells Maeve. Both women are now on their hands and knees, scrabbling through the bricks like terriers after rats, tossing the broken pieces of the house aside in their frantic attempt to get to the buried voice.

But the voice suddenly stops, and no amount of shouting will make it cry out again. Maeve paws through the rubble. A bomb shelter can just as easily become a grave, she thinks. Maybe it is safer to be out on the streets, in the eye of the storm. Maybe Jeremy would have died this evening if he hadn't been rushing through the streets with Harriet.

Harriet leans back on her heels, looks over at Maeve. "It's no use," she says. But Maeve just keeps going, and Harriet has to stumble across the pile of bricks and grab her by the arm to make her stop. "She's gone," she says.

Maeve lifts her hands from the warm bricks. She can't feel her fingertips. Her nails are torn and bleeding.

"Come here," says Harriet. "Come here." And she takes Maeve's hands in her own, covers them, holding them still.

Harriet is touched by Maeve's desire to save everyone. It reminds her of Jeremy's eagerness to help at the aid station. She starts to cry, sitting on top of the destroyed house, holding Maeve's hands in her own. She feels herself sway and settle, sway and settle, like a building hit by a blast. It's Maeve who has to help her up from the rubble.

———

"This is the passage," says Harriet. They have come to the bombed-out row of shops. "The Anderson shelter is just through here." She goes first down the alley and Maeve keeps close behind her. She is finding it hard to breathe.

The sky is lighter. Everything is more distinct, swims up to fill in the dark of the city.

The shelter has been hit. There's a huge hole in one side of it and the roof has exploded out; big ragged strips of metal shear up toward the sky. Maeve remembers the literature for the Anderson shelter saying that it would survive anything except a direct hit.

"No," says Maeve, and she breaks into a run, reaches the shelter first, and puts her head through the hole in the side. "Jeremy," she yells. "Jeremy."

The shelter is deserted. There is no one in it, just torn remnants from the bolt of chintz that Marjorie Hatton had used for bandages.

Harriet sits down on the ground outside the shelter, drawing her knees up to her chest and hugging them. She can't believe Jeremy is dead. He must be somewhere else.

All around her the sky is lightening. Harriet can see the broken beams and the hanging plaster from the backs of the bombed-out row of shops. The sky is grey and a thin drizzle is sieving down. She wraps her borrowed coat tighter around herself.

What if he never made it here but got lost on the way? What if, by the time he got here, the shelter was already bombed?

Maeve comes back out.

"We should try the hospital," says Harriet.

"Wouldn't it have been hit?"

"We should try anyway."

Harriet can feel the mist on her face, how it is starting to slide down the back of her neck. She remembers standing in the rain at Ypres, by that section of broken stone wall, how she knew so completely that Owen had died there. Here, she doesn't feel anything.

Maeve stands in front of Harriet. Her heart is beating so fast she can hear it as though it is beating outside her body.

"I want to go home," she says. "Will you take me?"

―――――――

Inside, Maeve's house is exactly as she left it, and she knows the moment they walk through the front door that Jeremy isn't there. Still, she looks around, races up the stairs two at a time to check the bedrooms.

When she comes back down she finds Harriet in the kitchen sitting at the table. Maeve walks into the room, accidentally kicking a potato that's lying on the floor. It rolls into the cabinet by the sink. She kicks another potato, on purpose, and it skids under the table, hitting the wall with a smack.

"He's not here."

"No," says Harriet. She didn't think he would be.

"What about my note? Did he find my note when you were here? Did he read it?"

"What note?" asks Harriet, and Maeve can see that the

kitchen is such a mess that her note, carefully placed on the kitchen table has disappeared, lifted into the air perhaps by a bomb blast and blown into some other part of the house.

Maeve leans against the door frame.

"Are you hungry?" asks Harriet.

"I hadn't thought about it."

"Should we eat something?" Harriet is hungry but doesn't want to make a point of it. She can tell how upset Maeve is. It feels petty to ask for a piece of bread.

Maeve moves over to the larder, finds some candles and lights them, sticking them to a saucer with the drips of hot wax. She brings them over to the table where Harriet sits. The light shivers up the wall when a bomb detonates.

She finds some cheese and biscuits and a tin of sardines. There are two bottles of ale on the larder floor and she brings these to the table as well.

"Helps with my drawing," she says as she slaps one of the bottles down in front of Harriet, making her jump.

Maeve takes a sliver of cheese and lays it carefully on top of a stale digestive biscuit. "Did Jeremy have a nap?"

"A nap?"

"His bed is unmade. I know I straightened it when I came back here from the pub."

It seems only good manners to lie.

"That was me," says Harriet. "After he left I had a bit of a rest."

They eat in silence for a while.

"Why did you let him go?" asks Maeve.

"He wanted to go. He wanted to help." Harriet pushes her plate away, her appetite suddenly gone. "I'm sorry," she says, and she gets up from the table and goes into the sitting room.

Maeve takes the plates over to the sink, stands there for a moment, remembering the old order of things—eat, wash up, dry the dishes with a linen tea towel, put the plates carefully back on the shelves. Everything has been broken into fragments by the bombing, even the slow chain of habit has come apart. Maeve hadn't realized how much her days had depended on an outside structure to support them.

She finds Harriet standing by the broken front window in the sitting room, staring out over the garden. The sky is lighter above the stone wall. Dawn is coming, and perhaps she is imagining it, but Maeve thinks the bombing is less frequent.

"Does it seem quieter to you?" she says to Harriet.

"Yes, I suppose it does." Harriet turns from the window. "I remember you," she says.

"From where?"

"We rode a bus together at the start of the last war. The first double-decker in Coventry."

Maeve looks hard at Harriet. She does remember the bus ride. She remembers the young woman who chased the bus through the streets with her so they could board. She remembers the tea, and the promise to return the next day. She remembers giving Harriet a sketch of the cathedral. But this woman bears little resemblance to the lively young woman she remembers.

"I wanted to come back," she says. "But it proved impossible."

"I waited," says Harriet. "I waited for everyone." She looks out over the stone wall, thinking of her flattened house and garden one street over. "That morning I met you, I had just been to the station to see my husband off to war."

"I remember."

"He died the next month. At Ypres." Harriet turns to Maeve. "Jeremy reminded me a little of Owen." She is quiet. "All he was trying to do tonight was to get back to you. He wanted to find you, make sure you were safe."

"Where shall we look for him now?" asks Maeve.

"I don't know."

There's a mist settling over the garden wall. Strangely, it almost seems like any other morning.

"Let's go back to where you started," says Maeve. "Let's go to the cathedral."

———————

The all-clear sounds when they're back on Broadgate. Almost immediately people appear again, emerging from shelters and cellars, from under their dining-room tables, from inside their fortified garden sheds. They come out into the street, brushing dust from their clothes and removing saucepans from their heads. They are like animals emerging from their burrows, blinking in the daylight, looking around as though seeing the world for the first time.

The air is still thick with dust, and there is the smell of gas hanging in the streets. There is also the smell of smouldering wood and the faint hiss of fire. Children rush about in their pyjamas and slippers, having gone into the shelters dressed for bed. An old man lies on a blanket near a gutted house, waiting to be picked up by an ambulance.

Maeve and Harriet stand in the street with the gathering crowd. Everyone looks at the burned-out shops, at the piles of brick and stone, the shattered glass crunching underfoot.

"I don't really feel alive," says Maeve, and Harriet knows what she means. The world they left is unrecognizable, not a place they want to inhabit. It feels like a sort of afterlife. They are their own ghosts.

The crowd of people stand for a while in the street and then they start to move together, to trickle down Broadgate, in the direction of the cathedral.

Harriet thinks of her descriptions. They must have burned up when the bomb fell on her house. There is nothing left of anything she wrote, and yet, walking down Broadgate, with the all-clear ringing in her ears, she finds that she remembers more of what she'd written than she thought.

For a week once, in springtime, Harriet watched a nest of wrens. She crouched on the verge beside the road and documented the activities of the family of birds in the hedgerow opposite. Several times during the week's surveillance she was mistaken for a tramp by passersby and told to move on. A child threw a rock at her from a bicycle, and she often lost the feeling in her legs from the awkward way she was forced to squat so the birds wouldn't notice her and be alarmed. She developed a rash from something scratchy on the verge.

She did her observation work on her lunch hour, hastily bolting her sandwiches on the walk out to the verge. The wrens came and went with a frequency she found disquieting, and, at the end of the week, when Harriet stayed late at the office to type up her description, she found her week's work had distilled down into a single sentence.

Flight is rhythmical, a sped-up version of the human heart perhaps.

What would she say about this moment? She looks around at the other people streaming down the centre of the road, at the ragged shells of buildings, some still smoking, at the fine mist falling over the city.

I have lost everything, and yet what I mind losing most is the acquaintance of the young man I just met tonight. How strange that is, and how liberating. Perhaps I will feel differently when this is over and I'm expected to return to some semblance of normal life. Perhaps then I will miss my flat, my clothes, the assorted books and paintings I have collected over the years.

Broadgate is a rubbish tip. The rain makes everything seem more desolate, although it also seems wrong that the sun should shine on this day. I can't help thinking in selfish terms—*There's the butcher's where I used to line up for bacon. There's the cinema where I would sometimes go*—but surely everyone is thinking in selfish terms today? Surely everyone is thinking about what they have lost, and what is perhaps still recoverable.

"That's where the church was," says Harriet. "We sheltered in the basement and then an unexploded bomb slid down the steps and we had to get out."

The church is now a broken heap of stone.

An ambulance wails. The vehicle weaves up the street, dodging piles of rubble. The crowd parts to let the ambulance through. A few people cheer as it wobbles past.

"Couldn't that have happened?" says Maeve. "Couldn't an ambulance have come by and evacuated the shelter? Couldn't Jeremy have gone with the injured people to some safer place?"

Harriet doesn't say anything. They didn't see an ambulance the whole time they were wandering about. It seems unlikely that one would have been able to get through the city at the height of the bombing. And how would the ambulance get to the shelter? The shelter was invisible from the street. But there seems no explanation as to where Jeremy is. If he did make it back to the aid station, and the aid station was hit soon after, Maeve's right, his body would still be there, as would the bodies of the injured people, some of whom, Harriet remembers, couldn't move. It's not as if she has seen anyone going around removing the dead from under their burial mounds of rubble.

If Harriet were to remake the world, how would she do it? Would she have a guidebook, something like *The Nomenclature of Colours,* to classify what exists on this new morning in Coventry? What made that book work so well was the constant reference to nature, how the natural world was used to define colour, to ground it. With so much of the city destroyed, what could be used in place of nature? Memory, thinks Harriet. The book she would write would be a catalogue of lost things.

———————

As they get closer to the cathedral, the crowd pushes in on them. Everyone seems to be instinctively headed for the same place. The cathedral is the heart of the city, and it seems natural to Harriet that they are all be tumbling back toward it on the morning after the bombing.

Maeve grabs hold of Harriet's sleeve. "I don't want to lose you," she says.

"You won't lose me."

They are almost at the cathedral, but there are so many people blocking them that Harriet can't see the building. She looks up for the spire, sees nothing but the head of the man in front of her and knows that the cathedral has been gutted.

There is nothing left of the roof. It has collapsed into the centre of the building, and the walls have crumbled. The windows are gone, but the window arches remain. Smoke is still trickling from the beams. They jostle nearer, Harriet actively pushing through the jam of people ahead of them.

"Look," says Maeve, pointing upward, and Harriet looks up to see that someone has tied two of the charred beams together in the shape of a cross and hung it over the altar.

It seems as if all of Coventry is in the ruined cathedral. Some people are weeping openly, some walk along with their heads bowed. The men have removed their hats. The children are silent. Everyone seems dazed, stumbling forward over the rubble that fills the space. The ground feels hot through Harriet's shoes, and much of it is impassable. As they get closer to the altar, Harriet can see that someone has written *Father Forgive* behind the cross of burned wood. Around the altar are placed glass jars with wildflowers in them.

It seems impossible that Harriet was once standing on the roof of this building, that she walked up and down, under the stars and above the frosted ground.

Maeve feels as though she's going to collapse.

"Wait," she says to Harriet. "Stop." The cheerful optimism and bravery has drained out of her since entering the cathedral. She feels afraid.

"I need a minute," she says, and she and Harriet walk over to the side of the cathedral, out of the moving crowd.

Harriet has a hand on Maeve's arm to steady her, turns to look at the crowd gathering behind them, thinking that perhaps Jeremy might have made his way back here too, that he might be standing in this mass of people, recalling how he once stood on the roof, how he paced with Harriet under the heavens, guardians of the city. In that moment when Harriet turns to look for Jeremy, she sees Marjorie Hatton. She's moving slowly forward in the middle of the throng.

It is harder to push against the crowd than to be carried along by it, and Harriet struggles to fight her way through to Marjorie. But soon she is there, and has the nurse by the sleeve.

"Marjorie," she says. "Remember me? Harriet Marsh?"

Marjorie Hatton looks confused, and then recognizes her. "I'm glad you made it," she says.

"Jeremy," Harriet says. "Do you know what happened to Jeremy?"

Marjorie lowers her head, and Harriet feels cold with fear.

"He found a bus," says Marjorie. "A sort of ambulance bus, on his way back to my shelter. I mean, it was a regular bus that had turned into an ambulance, with a driver who was taking the wounded to hospital. We were loading my patients into the bus. Jeremy had just gone back for the last one when he was hit by the blast."

"Hit?"

"Killed," says Marjorie Hatton. "We pulled him into the bus and took him to hospital with the others, but he was already dead. I'm so sorry."

———————

Harriet stands still in the centre of the cathedral. All around her people move forward to look at the altar, to place flowers in the glass jars there.

Jeremy, like Owen, has left her. She shouldn't have let him go. She should have kept him with her, kept him safe. She puts her hand into her pocket, finds the miniature fire that he gave her. It is cold to the touch.

In this grey morning, the tide of living people rises around her.

Harriet can see Maeve leaning against the wall. She begins to move forward, toward Maeve, already shaping the words she knows she has to say.

And then, right in front of Maeve, Harriet sees her neighbour, Wendell Mumby. He is standing talking to two men under what used to be the chancel roof and is now just a patch of grey sky. Wendell Mumby has his sleeves rolled up and his good tweed cap on. He throws his head back as Harriet is watching and laughs at something she can't hear.

———————

Maeve sees Harriet moving back toward her through the crowd. Harriet is moving with purpose. She has something to tell Maeve, and Maeve can see by the look on Harriet's face that she knows something.

She remembers watching Jeremy leave the house yesterday afternoon for his fire-watching duties, how she had stood at the window in the sitting room as he sauntered up the road. He liked wearing the uniform. It put a bounce in his step. At the corner, confident his mother was watching, he turned and bowed. *Cheeky monkey,* she had thought.

Harriet is there, has taken Maeve's hand in her own, is already saying the words that Maeve will have to carry with her forever. But she isn't listening. She's high up, on the top of a double-decker bus, flying through the streets of Coventry. The sun is warm on Maeve's hands where they grip the seat in front, and the spirited girl she has just met is beside her, whooping with joy. It seems to Maeve that her life is perfect. There is nothing else to want.

MAY 26, 1962

Harriet steps into the new cathedral. She has taken a train to Coventry, up from her small flat by the sea in Newhaven, and she is tired from the journey. She has come straight from the station, for fear of being late for the ceremony, and hasn't had a chance to look around the city yet. But she can see that it is unrecognizable. In the twenty-two years since she was last here, the main part of Coventry has been completely rebuilt. Harriet finds the new architecture ugly, certainly no replacement for the seventeenth-century buildings that used to occupy the space.

Coventry Cathedral was the only cathedral in Britain to be destroyed in the war. The decision to rebuild it happened the day after the bombing, but it has taken all these years to make that decision a reality. The new cathedral is modern, with great sheer walls inspired by Norman architecture, but which remind Harriet of all the other modern buildings she has driven past in the taxi from the train station. What has drawn her to the new cathedral is that they have incorporated the ruins of the old cathedral in the building of the new, have attached the two, so that one can walk through the splendour of the rebuilt church and then out to the roofless shell of the old St. Michael's.

Harriet gets tired easily these days, even though she tries to keep herself fit by striding along the beach or, on good days, walking up onto the top of the cliffs to stumble along the backs of the hills. She has travelled up from Sussex and she is glad that all that is required of her today is to enter the cathedral and sit down for the opening ceremonies.

The inside is beautiful, much more beautiful than she could have imagined from the exterior. Harriet slides into a pew at the back of the church and spends the entire length of the ceremony looking at the magnificent stained-glass window. The blue in it is a colour so deep it seems to have drifted up from the bottom of the ocean to roost there, on the wall of this church. Coventry blue.

———

When Harriet steps into the old cathedral, it is as though no time has passed at all. The debris has long been cleared from the floor and the stones are swept clean. But everything else is the same as it was the morning after the bombing. The window arches are still empty of glass. The roof is still gone. There are benches placed discreetly around the outside walls, and Harriet moves to one of these and sits down.

There is the wall that Maeve was leaning against when Harriet had to tell her that her son was dead. There is the place in the sky where she once walked up and down on the roof with Jeremy Fisher.

It has taken Harriet all this time, twenty-two years, to try to write about that night, and she hasn't done it properly yet. She has traded her descriptions for poems, and has had some success publishing them. She has a book that did modestly well in the reviews, and she is working hard on another one. Her poems have been included in anthologies and broadcast on the wireless. What Harriet has been searching for in her poems are the words to make sense of what happened on that night in November all those years ago.

She keeps in loose touch with Maeve Fisher. *I promise I will always let you know where I am* is what Maeve said, and she has been as good as her word. She moves around a lot. Right now she is living on the Aran Islands off the coast of Ireland. *The light is beautiful,* she had written to Harriet recently. *And the strict, shadowed cliffs rising up from the sea are exactly how I feel.*

There are a lot of people milling about in the old cathedral. Almost as many people as there were on the morning after the bombing. There are some in their sixties and seventies, some who, like Harriet, must have been there the night of the raid. They don't talk much, just walk slowly around the walls, or sit on the benches, like Harriet, watching the crowd.

Harriet still looks for Jeremy. Everywhere she goes she scans the faces, searching him out. It has become a habit and she can't rest until she has done it now, looking quickly and anxiously at the visitors to the new cathedral. Of course, he isn't here. But there is something in the act of looking for him that keeps his memory alive for Harriet. In the end, that is what she has been left, and this is her way of keeping faith.

The day is a lovely one, the air soft and the sun sliding in and out of the clouds. Harriet likes this time of year, how long the light stays in the evenings, how green the fields are. She closes her eyes to feel the warmth of the sun on her face, opens them and sees, falling through the air above the cathedral, a single swallow. It seems delighted with all the space, climbing and diving, scissoring through the open window arches.

———————

Harriet buys a postcard of the new cathedral, and on her way back to the station in the taxi she writes to Maeve. They are not the right words to give her, not yet, but they are closer than she has ever been before.

———————

Maeve walks away from the jetty. She heads uphill, to her cottage, but when she reaches the front gate she hesitates and keeps going, up toward the fields sewn sloppily together by the low stone walls that cover the island. In the pocket of her bulky cardigan is the bundle of mail she has collected from the boat. There is a postcard from Harriet in with the letters and bills. It seems wrong to go indoors, into her dark kitchen to read the card. She will find somewhere to sit down, in the sun, so she can fully appreciate Harriet's words.

The village on Innismor where Maeve lives is little more than a scattering of houses arranged haphazardly around the small harbour. The houses seem to have been lifted there by the sea, their white walls set like bleached bones among the rocks.

Maeve stops on the road to catch her breath, turns and sees the houses flashing white behind her. Beyond them, she can see the mail boat lurching away from the jetty, heading back across the Atlantic to Galway.

Maeve had expected Tom to be on the boat. That is why she had gone down to the harbour, to meet her husband. But Tom probably got talking with someone, or tried to squeeze in one more errand before the boat left, and arrived on the Galway dock just in time to watch the battered black hull of the mail boat pushing out to sea.

It is not the first time this has happened, and because

it has happened so many times before, Maeve isn't overly surprised or worried. Tom is dependable in his vagrancy. He will show up tomorrow, or the day after, cheerfully apologetic, bounding spryly up from the beach with stories and his canvas bag filled with food and some small present for Maeve from his time in the city.

Maeve had not expected to marry and be happy. She had not expected to meet someone late in life, someone who liked to move around as much as she did. But Tom is even more of a nomad. He is originally from America, but has spent most of his life elsewhere. He has lived throughout South America and Europe and has come to the Aran Islands because, like Maeve, he can live cheaply there, and he loves the way the light shovels in off the Atlantic.

Tom is a painter. He has fashioned a studio out of the small barn behind their cottage. He wakes late and spends much of his day in the studio. In the evenings he and Maeve read, or walk to the one pub on the island to have a pint. He never minds company when he works, and Maeve likes to go into the studio to watch him paint. He has an energy when he works that she finds intoxicating. In some ways he reminds her of Jeremy, of the concentration Jeremy used to have when he set himself a task.

Where once Maeve would have found the resemblance painful, now there is some comfort in it.

Maeve begins to walk up the road again. Slowly the

houses fall away and she is walking with green fields on either side of her. Each field is bordered by a wall made of the stones that had been cleared from the field. The walls have no gates. If a farmer wants to shift his cows and sheep to another field, he simply removes some of the stones from a section of wall, replacing them when the animals are safely away in the next field.

This is another reason why Maeve likes living on the Aran Islands. Everything here is as it always was. There is no electricity, no motor cars. Many of the people on the islands still speak Gaelic. The lack of change is reassuring, though Maeve wonders if she will be able to survive the harshness of the conditions into her very old age. But Tom is already talking about moving them to Spain; though Maeve loves the starkness of Innismor, the thought of the Spanish sun warming her bones is tempting.

The road is steep, the centre of the island being much higher than the sea that twists all around it. Maeve has to pause frequently in her climb. She hasn't really minded becoming old, but it still surprises her that she can't move as fluently as she once did.

Her heart is whirring fast inside her chest.

This is probably far enough.

She settles down with her back against a wall and takes the bundle of mail from her pocket. The postcard from Harriet slips easily out of the pile.

It is a picture of the new cathedral. It looks nothing like the old one—all sheer and modern—but Maeve's hands start shaking at the sight of it. She takes a deep breath. The stones from the wall are warm against her back, warm through the thick wool of her jumper.

This is what she and Harriet do—pass the memory of that night in November 1940 back and forth between them. Harriet will send Maeve a poem. Maeve will send Harriet a drawing. Where once Maeve drew the world around her to navigate it, now she draws only the images from the night when Coventry fell, and when Jeremy died. Drawing something used to be a way for her to record what was being lost, a way to slow the moment down long enough to get a good look at what was moving just out of reach. Now it is purely a way to hold on to what she has lost.

Every act is an act of mourning, thinks Maeve. Every moment is about leaving the previous moment behind.

She has drawn the cramped, dark pub cellar where she sheltered at the beginning of the bombing. She has drawn Jeremy's soldiers in frozen march across his bedroom window ledge. She has drawn Harriet's hands cradling her own when they were atop that pile of rubble where they had heard the woman's voice calling out to be saved. And she has drawn the metal rib cage of the Anderson shelter with the ragged hole torn through its side.

But even though this exchange of memory is a way for Harriet and Maeve to keep something of Jeremy alive, it is always a shock to remember. It is always a shock to get a card or letter from Harriet, and to have to open herself, again, to the horrors of that night.

For a while, after the night of the bombing, Maeve believed that Harriet had simply been a guide through the ruined city to her son. But the longer her association with her continues, the more Maeve has come to realize that something else must have happened the night Coventry fell. Harriet has never said, and Maeve can't bring herself to ask, but she assumes now that Harriet and Jeremy were briefly lovers. Why else would Harriet keep this vigil with her? Once Maeve might have minded this, but now she is only grateful that her child was loved during his last night on earth.

The sun is making Maeve's eyes water. She runs her thumb along the straight edges of the postcard. Down one side, along another, as if they were streets she was walking.

The night still makes no sense, no matter how hard Maeve looks at it, no matter what pictures she is able to pull from the wreckage. But thank god for Harriet Marsh, she thinks. Thank god that in the loneliest of griefs, she is not alone.

She turns the card over and begins to read the words Harriet has sent to her.

ACKNOWLEDGEMENTS

I would like to thank my agent, Frances Hanna, and my editors, Phyllis Bruce and Amy Cherry, for their work and wisdom in shaping this story.

I used many books and accounts that detailed the events of November 14, 1940, but the following were particularly useful: *The Story of the Destruction of Coventry Cathedral* by Provost R.T. Howard; *Moonlight Sonata: The Coventry Blitz, 14/15 November 1940* compiled and edited by Tim Lewis; *The Coventry We Have Lost* (volumes I and II) by Albert Smith and David Fry; the pictorial records *Coventry at War* and *Memories of Coventry*, both presented by Alton Douglas in conjunction with the *Coventry Evening Telegraph*; and *Air Raid: The Bombing of Coventry, 1940* by Norman Longmate. My descriptions of the burning city are based on the accounts of the citizens of Coventry, as well as on eyewitness accounts of the bombing of Baghdad.

The guidebook Harriet references in the 1919 section of this novel is the illustrated Michelin guide from that same year, called *Ypres and the Battles for Ypres*. The letter from Owen Marsh is an actual letter from my grandfather, Dudley d'Herbez Humphreys, who fought in the trenches at Ypres in 1914. References to *Werner's Nomenclature of Colours,* by Abraham Gottlob Werner, correspond to the 1821 edition published by Patrick Syme.

Thanks to the following people for seeing me through the writing of this book: Mary Louise Adams, Elizabeth Christie, Craig Dale, Carol Drake, Melanie Dugan, Sue Goyette, Elizabeth Greene, Anne Hardcastle, Cathy Humphreys, Paul Kelley, Hugh LaFave, Paula Leger, Susan Lord, Barb Mainguy, Bruce Martin, Daintry Norman, Joanne Page, Elizabeth Ruth, Su Rynard, Diane Schoemperlen, Glenn Stairs.

Special thanks to Valerie Ashford. I couldn't have done this without you.